NIGHT IN FUNLAND

AND OTHER STORIES FROM
LITERARY CAVALCADE

NIGHT IN FUNLAND

AND OTHER STORIES FROM
LITERARY CAVALCADE

Edited by Jerome Brondfield

SBS SCHOLASTIC BOOK SERVICES
New York Toronto London Auckland Sydney

ACKNOWLEDGMENTS

ANTAEUS by Borden Deal from **Southwest Review**, © 1961 by Southern Methodist University Press. Reprinted by permission of Paul R. Reynolds, Inc.

AS BEST HE CAN from THE BRIDES OF SOLOMON AND OTHER STORIES by Geoffrey Household, © 1958 by Geoffrey Household. Reprinted by permission of Atlantic-Little, Brown and Co.

AUGUST HEAT from THE BEAST WITH FIVE FINGERS by William Fryer Harvey. Copyright 1947 by E. P. Dutton & Co., Inc. Reprinted by permission of E. P. Dutton & Co., Inc. and J. M. Dent & Sons Ltd.

CONTENTS OF A DEAD MAN'S POCKET from THE THIRD LEVEL by Jack Finney, © 1957 by Jack Finney. Reprinted by permission of the Harold Matson Co., Inc.

EXCHANGE OF MEN by Howard Nemerov and S. R. Johnson, © 1963 by Story Magazine, Inc. Reprinted by permission of the authors.

FLOWERS FOR ALGERNON by Daniel Keyes, © 1959 by Daniel Keyes. Reprinted by permission of Robert P. Mills, Literary Agent.

FOUR O'CLOCK by Price Day. Copyright 1958 by H. S. D. Publications, Inc. From ANTHOLOGY OF SHORT STORIES, Vol. 8. Reprinted by permission of Thomas Ober Associates.

THE MOST DANGEROUS GAME by Richard Connell, copyright 1924 by Richard Connell. Copyright renewed 1952 by Louise Fox Connell. Reprinted by permission of Brandt & Brandt.

NIGHT IN FUNLAND by William Peden. From the **New Mexico Quarterly**, © 1960 by the University of New Mexico Press. Reprinted by permission of the author.

ONE ORDINARY DAY, WITH PEANUTS by Shirley Jackson, © 1955 by Shirley Jackson. First published in **The Magazine of Fantasy and Science Fiction**. Reprinted by permission of Brandt & Brandt.

THE SEA GULLS by Elias Venezis, © 1955 by Atlantic Monthly Company. Reprinted by permission of the author.

TOO EARLY SPRING by Stephen Vincent Benet from THE SELECTED WORKS OF STEPHEN VINCENT BENET, published by Holt, Rinehart and Winston, Inc. Copyright 1933 by The Butterick Co. Copyright renewed © 1961 by Rosemary Carr Benet. Reprinted by permission of Brandt & Brandt.

THE VERTICAL LADDER from THE STORIES OF WILLIAM SANSOM, © 1960 by William Sansom. Reprinted by permission of Atlantic-Little, Brown and Co.

4th printing . . . . December 1969

Printed in the U.S.A.

FOREWORD

The task of choosing a select list of the best short stories reprinted in *Literary Cavalcade* was one which, from every apparent angle, turned out to be an embarrassment of riches. How do you winnow the "best from the best"? *Cavalcade*, first of all, is a magazine for students in advanced English classes and creative writing courses; over the years, its editors have chosen fiction from thousands of the finest short stories previously appearing in print from dozens of sources. To pick from this total number just enough for a collection of this size was almost presumptuous. But, so be it. We relied on the anthologist's privilege of falling back, unashamedly, on his personal taste — at the same time, of course, striving for variety of subject, mood, and style. The stories in this book fall into that over-all pattern.

One of them, since it was reprinted in *LC*, has been reprinted widely elsewhere, and has virtually become a classic of contemporary short literature, read and reread by students, teachers, and parents. Its title: "Flowers for Algernon," and the title gives you very little clue to the story — a stunning story which has, by their own admission, left tears in the eyes of many readers.

There are others almost as memorable in their impact, as some of the world's greatest short story writers weave their individual magic through the pages of this richly entertaining collection.

Suspense . . .? Begin "August Heat" or "Contents of the Dead Man's Pocket" and try to stop. Whimsy . . .? You'll regard "One Ordinary Day, with Peanuts" as the most delightful premise you've come across in a long time. Technique . . .? Analyze "As Best He Can," and note it is a story written entirely in dialogue, without a single word of narrative.

Every story in this collection has something special to commend it. We think you will come to treat it as a private literary treasure that will reward you over and over again.

JEROME BRONDFIELD, EDITOR
LITERARY CAVALCADE

CONTENTS

This, we believe, is one of the greatest
horror stories ever written in the English
language. Not for its horror, per se, because it isn't at all that gruesome. But for
sheer concept and the development of the
idea, it has few, if any, peers.

"I dare you!" How many times have you
heard that? How many times have you
heard the challenge flung at you, or
somebody you know? Here is a haunting
instance of how hollow and meaningless
and catastrophic it can be for both the
challenger and the challenged, told with
great feeling and drama.

It seemed the old lighthouse keeper had
little to live for except his beloved birds.
Just how much they meant to him is the
essence of this mystical, bittersweet story
of an old man and the sea around him.

A farmboy is transplanted to the big city
and yearns for a plot of dirt to grow
things. After convincing his city pals
they can haul dirt to the top of a factory
roof and turn it into a garden, he involves
you in a story that will make you feel
you are an eyewitness to an event you
will never forget.

> An outstanding example of stream-of-consciousness story-telling technique. Virtually the entire tale is seen flashing through the mind of a man trapped on a building ledge high above the street. The way the suspense builds, the reader will sweat as much as the man outside the window.

> The first thing you should notice is the unique form of this story. It is written entirely in dialogue. There isn't a line of narrative in it. Beyond that, it is a sardonic gem that will keep you rooted to every word—and give you a wry chuckle at its conclusion.

> If there is one word to describe this story it is "poignant." No, make that *achingly* poignant. It is a story for the young to hold up to their elders and say, accusingly: "This time you are wrong!"

NIGHT IN FUNLAND
WILLIAM PEDEN

THEY DROVE SLOWLY down the highway that cut cleanly through the desert, past the glittering motels with their swimming pools of pale blue water, past the shops of pink or green or azure adobe. In the humming light of the mercury-vapor lamps, the child was a gnome in a pool of color, the shadows beneath her eyes sooty in the darkness that had overrun the mesa. The father reached over and patted her hand. She squeezed his and edged closer toward him.

"Are you sure this is the way, Daddy?"

"Of course it is, Amanda, don't you remember?"

"Well, yes, sort of, but I thought maybe it was the other way."

"The other way is east, goosie," he said; "we go west. Look, in a minute, at the next stop light, we will see the wheel, and then you will remember."

At the intersection he slowed down as the traffic light clicked from green to amber and then to red.

"Look," he pointed at the rosy sky; "over there; can't you see the top of the Ferris wheel?"

She squealed with delight; then the light changed and they left the shining highway, and in darkness that was like a sudden plunge into unknown waters turned onto a bumpy dirt road.

"Can we get there this way?" Amanda asked. "Does this road go through?"

"Don't sorry; sure it does, honey. You just wait."

Then they were pulling into the tumbleweed-speckled parking lot. He switched off the motor, and turned off the lights, and went around and opened her door. Amanda came out slowly, and she smiled up at her spare, slightly stooped father.

"This is fun," she said. She reached for his hand and they walked beneath the arch that spelled out F-U-N-L-A-N-D in winking colored lights. It was a clean, bright place, no leg shows, no wheels of fortune, no freak tents with green-ish two-headed babies in discolored alcohol-filled jars; a clean bright place on the mesa, bounded by a miniature railroad with puffing steam engine and train of cars. They could hear the whistle now at the far dark end of the park, faraway and thin and clear, and Amanda tugged at his hand again. He wanted to pull her close to him and kiss her and pat her thin hair and tell her how glad he was that she was so much better and they could go on a spree together as they had in the old days, and he patted her hand and buttoned the top button of her sweater.

"Let's sit down a little," he said. His heart was thumping and the palms of his hands were damp.

"Oh, Daddy," she said, "not now."

"You must rest a minute," he insisted; "you must remember this is the first time. . . ."

They sat down on the bench by the small depot, and the train with its bell clanging and its whistle shrilling and its headlights stabbing at the night swung around the turn, and stopped quietly almost in front of them. The engineer, a teen-aged boy crouching precariously on the tender, got up to stretch his legs while the young passengers spilled from the coaches.

"What shall we do first?" the father asked. "Do you want to ride the train?"

"I'd like a snowball first," she said. Children were climbing on and off the train like monkeys, and he thought there were too many of them, and if one of them coughed on her or something it wouldn't help her, certainly, to catch a cold or something just now. She walked ahead of him slowly, a trace of her old jauntiness in the blue toreadors with the white bows tied neatly just below her knees and the white-trimmed cap on her dark head, past the pool with its boats floating in the oil-dark water, and the enclosure where the ponies awaited their riders, and the clanking fury of the scenic railway.

"This is the nicest park ever," he said, and

squeezed her hand. "I have never been in a nicer park, have you, Amanda?"

"No," she said; "it is the nicest ever."

At the refreshment booth he ordered two snowballs, with grape flavoring. The efficient girl in her starched white uniform pushed a button and there was a whirling sound, and the ice as white and fine as snow poured through a vent, and the girl scooped it up and, expertly, without touching it by hand, transferred it into paper cups, and then she squirted thick dark purple fluid onto the ice, and it was suddenly, magically, like a sunset, transformed into a violet delight, and she smiled and passed the cups over the counter.

"Keep your fingers out of it," he said to Amanda.

They rested on a bench, and tilted the cups to their lips, and the sweet ice gushed into their mouths.

"Isn't it good?" Amanda said. "It gets sweeter as it goes down."

"Yes," he said, and thought how few things were sweeter as they go down, and he squeezed his cup and the fluid was bright and clean in his mouth.

"This is the nicest park there is," he said again.

"Yes," she said, and drained at her snowball with a sucking, bubbling sound. She thrust her thin fingers into the cup to extract the last sweet dregs. Roughly he snatched out her hand and slapped her hard, and cried he had told her to keep her fingers out of it, and did she want to get sick all over again. She flushed and he felt as if he had kicked her, and he pulled her close to him and kissed and stroked her hair; her thinness was like a blow.

"I am so sorry, honey," he said, "but I have been worried about you. You must not mind when I act like this. It is only because I do not want you to get sick again, ever."

She slowly turned her head toward him, and tried to smile, and he took out his monogrammed handkerchief and brushed at the corners of her eyes.

"Now how do you feel?" he asked, and when she said she felt fine he wanted to shout and dance and sing. He held her hand as they walked away from the refreshment booth while the starched girl squinted at him, and they walked slowly over the hard-packed grayish dirt. There was very little dust, he thought with satisfaction; he had never known a place like Funland to be so clean and orderly.

Amanda suddenly broke from his grasp.

"Oh," she cried, and ran toward a large brightly lighted cage near an open place where baby tanks puffed and grunted.

"Look," she called. "Oh, Daddy, look."

In the bright clean cage, littered with scooter, tricycle, rubber balls, trapeze, and punching bag, a young chimpanzee sat in a baby's high chair, munching at a banana.

"Rollo," the sign atop the cage read. "Just Recently Arrived from the Belgian Congo Region of West Africa. A two-year-old chimpanzee . . . just four and a half months in captivity."

Daintily Rollo nibbled, breaking off small

chunks with his long-haired, tiny-nailed hands and placing the fruit meticulously in a mouth like the furnace door of the small train that was again circling the far, dark end of the grounds, emerging from its tunnel with a triumphant toot and jangle. The chimpanzee finished his treat, placed the parachute of limp skin on the tray of his chair and wiped his hands on scarlet trousers. Amanda screamed with delight and Rollo swung with dedicated grace to land noiselessly on the floor with flat tennis-shoe-clad feet. With strong, pink-palmed, beautiful hands he grasped the bars of his cage and gazed at the child with stone-dark eyes, like small pools of night in his clean, tanned face, and he opened his great lips, and smiled.

Amanda clapped her hands and Rollo whirled and leaped to the rope which spanned the cage; hand over hand, he swung from one end of the cage to the other. By ones and twos people approached, laughing and chatting, and Rollo again dropped like a sunbeam to the floor. His trainer, a gentle, patient man with a limp and a dangling cigarette and a face too much like Rollo's to be a coincidence, reached for the roller skates hanging on the wall and attached them to the chimpanzee's high-topped tennis shoes. He held his hand, and Rollo glided noiselessly on his well-oiled skates, skating surely and competently and enjoying himself.

When a man climbed clumsily over the low iron railing in front of the cage and tossed a few pieces of popcorn between the bars, Rollo stumbled and almost fell. The attendant reached quickly for the chimpanzee's hand and frowned at the intruder. Amanda turned upon the popcorn thrower, a fat man in a bilge-colored nylon sport shirt.

"You've frightened him," she said in sudden fury. "You've frightened him."

In anger the fat man threw another handful of popcorn between the bars, and the trainer sadly shook his head. Still holding Rollo by the hand, he led him to the high chair and pulled a switch, and all the lights in the cage went out. Rollo sat alone, his yellow shirt and scarlet trousers and sneakered feet now gray in the darkness.

"Who does that guy think he is, anyways?" the fat man said. "It's only a monkey."

He grabbed his fat child, a child with a face like a rutabaga, and disappeared.

"What a horrid, nasty man," Amanda said. "Can't we see Rollo again? Won't he come out again?"

"Maybe later," the father said. "Maybe later."

"Besides," she said, "he's not a monkey. He's a chimpanzee, an anth . . . anthropoid, isn't he, Daddy?"

"That's right," he said. "He's not a monkey, he's an anthropoid, and maybe he'll come out later anyhow."

Amanda walked away, but soon stopped at the foot of the Ferris wheel. She gazed upward at its swift smoothness, sparkling, a small circle of lights winking near the hub, and a larger circle glowing in the middle, and the whole great machine alive with an outline of red and blue and green neon tubing, flashing as the twelve carriages, one red and another black, swam miraculously into the cool dry blackness of the starless night, some carriages swinging empty, in another two teen-aged girls singing "Oklahoma," in others a father and a white-faced, popeyed infant, a young man and a girl, their arms locked around each other as they soared from the light to the darkness, and two boys clowning and roaring. The operator squeezed the griphandle of the lever and pushed it and the engine slowed down, and the wheel came to a silent stop. There was a sudden, almost reverent hush, and a squeal of terrified delight from the occupants of the carriage at the very top of the wheel swinging coldly in the dark, and then the voices of the girls singing "Oklahoma" clear and faraway and miles and miles away in the thin cold air at the top of the wheel, and miles away from the hard gray ground and the prancing merry-go-round horses with their flaring orange nostrils and white champing cannibal teeth and the refreshment stand with the efficient girl in her starched white uniform. The operator stepped on a pedal, and a landing platform slid close to the carriage; the attendant lifted the bar and the occupants stepped down.

"Must we ride this now, Amanda?" the father asked.

"Oh, yes," she said, and edged her way toward the entrance. "Can I?" she said, and squeezed his hand, and her dark eyes glistened, "Oh, can I go all alone like you promised when I was sick?"

"Let me go with you," he said.

"Don't be a meanie," she said. "Please, Daddy, remember you promised."

"All right," he said. "All right, but you must be very, very careful. You must promise to sit right in the middle of the bar all the time. Do you promise?"

"Brownie's honor," she said and held up her hand, palm outward and three fingers aloft in a half salute. She hugged him, and he lowered his head and she brushed his cheek with a quick kiss.

The wheel stopped again, and he gave her her money and said loudly, "Give it to the man." He looked at the operator like a fellow-conspirator suddenly catching in a great crowd the long-anticipated signal, and again he said loudly, "If you do not sit right in the middle and hold the bar tightly I shall ask the attendant to stop the wheel."

"Oh, Daddy," she said. The operator smiled when she gave him the money, and placed her firmly in the very middle of the carriage, clicking the protective bar into place with special emphasis as though to say I understand the way you feel. Do not worry.

Amanda sat very straight in her seat and gripped the iron bar. The operator pushed the lever slowly forward, and the wheel rose noiselessly. Amanda smiled from her perch as the operator again pulled back the lever, and the wheel stopped and an aged man and wife emerged from their carriage as though from the floor of the ocean.

Again, the operator pushed the lever, and the wheel began to turn. The father ran back a few feet; he could see Amanda, tiny, disappearing into the darkness. He hoped the operator would not halt the wheel with Amanda's carriage at the summit. His mouth tightened as he thought of her, up there alone in the dark. He saw the crouching mountains, a ragged darkness palpable against the blue-black of the night, and the city swimming in a blob of red and blue and green and orange and white lights, while to the west naked and blue the desert scattered its bones to the ends of the vanished watershed. Then Amanda in a black carriage outlined with green neon swept past him, and smiled and was gone. He started to wave, but checked his arm, not wanting her to take her hands from the iron bar to reply. Then, in what seemed an instant, she came by him again, and he winked at her reassuringly before her carriage swam upward into the darkness. He looked at the sturdy iron wheel and the concrete foundation. This was no fly-by-night carnival, but a permanent operation, thank heaven, he thought; thousands of people rode the safe, sturdy wheel each season. Again Amanda was smiling when her carriage flashed by, and he lighted a cigarette and smiled conspiratorially at the operator in his white overalls, a sensible man with one foot resting nonchalantly near the flywheel of the generator.

He counted the carriages as they glided before his line of vision, one red then one black, then another red and another black. He awaited the passage of Amanda's carriage which he must have missed while he was lighting his cigarette. Suddenly, painfully, a hard ball of fear exploded in his throat.

This is absurd, he thought. He forced himself to stand still and look with studied calm at the swiftly turning wheel. What had been the color of the tubing which outlined Amanda's carriage? Green? No, red. Surely not red on red, or was it a black carriage?

The wheel made several more swift, noiseless circuits, and still he could not see the pale smiling face of Amanda. His hands shook and sweat drenched his back and upper legs. With an effort as conscious and deliberate as holding his breath under water he controlled himself. This is ridiculous, he thought. This is an optical illusion. He said to himself, I will count each carriage very carefully as it goes past, and then I will see her, and soon the wheel will stop, and she will get out, and we will have a very good laugh about this.

He counted the carriages as they glided swiftly before his eyes. First a red with an old man, then two empties, then a black with two grinning nob-headed boys, then a red with the girls now singing "Oh, What a Beautiful Morning," then an empty, then another red, and his heart suddenly reared like a geyser only to sink hideously; it was not Amanda, but a much older child. Then a man and a child and two more empties, then a red with a mother and a baby followed by a black with a soldier and a girl, then another red with an old man, the same hideous old man he'd begun counting with, and with a cry like an animal's he leaped over the low steel railing and clutched at the attendant's arm.

"Stop it," he said; "stop the wheel." The attendant frowned, then smiled, and squeezed the handle of the lever, and pulled back the lever, and an empty black carriage swung like a dry leaf above his head.

"My daughter," he gasped, "the little one with the black hair," but two snotty-nosed boys pushed their way between him and the operator, poking out their hands with the money in them, and climbed into the carriage snickering and guffawing and wolfing popcorn.

"For the love of God," he cried, and the popcorn-eaters looked at him as though he were an ape in a straw hat. "Where is my daughter? I think it is time you let the little girl off. The one with the black hair. You remember."

"Yes, sir," the attendant said, and smiled. Relief flowed through him; he slapped the operator heartily on the back.

"I lost sight of her for a moment," he said. "In the dark. My eyes. It gave me a turn for a moment."

The operator nodded, and pushed the lever, and the next carriage empty, swung past, and he stopped the wheel at the next to let the mother and baby out. The baby had wet its diaper and a dark stain overspread the mother's breast like a wound. Then there was the carriage with the soldier and the girl, and they leaned out and yelled whatsthematterwhyduyuhkeepstoppinthewheel? Then another empty and one in red with the old man, and he lost count. "Amanda," he screamed; his voice was like a ship sinking darkly.

"Amanda," he screamed again, and the attendant stopped the wheel and came toward him and he was no longer smiling. People converged upon him; he was the center of a whirling funnel of blank paper faces.

"Oh, God," he cried. "Where are you, baby?"

The children in the toy train, again making its sliding halt before the depot, leaned over the edges of the coaches and looked questioningly at the Ferris wheel glowing in the distance. "Amanda," the father cried, and the sound tore and twisted its way above the clanking of the scenic railway and the put-put-put of the merry-go-round.

Noiselessly the curtains of the clean cage parted, and the lights flowed on, and Rollo climbed quietly down from his high chair. He listened intently to the wild broken cries in the night. Then he pressed his tan face against the bars and gazed with comprehending eyes at the dark figure with uplifted head outlined like a corpse against the spokes of the great wheel blazing in the night.

4 O'CLOCK
PRICE DAY

THE HANDS OF THE ALARM CLOCK on the table in front of Mr. Crangle stood at 3:47 on a summer afternoon.

"You're wrong about that, you know," he said, not taking his eyes from the face of the clock. "You're quite wrong, Pet, as I have explained to you often enough before. The moral angle presents no difficulties at all."

The parrot, in the cage hanging above him, cocked her head and looked down with a hard, cold, reptilian eye, an ancient eye, an eye older by age upon age than the human race.

She said, "Nut."

Mr. Crangle, his eye still on the clock, took a peanut from a cracked bowl at his elbow and held it above his head, to the bars of the cage. Pet clutched it in a leathery claw. The spring-steel muscles opened the horny beak. She clinched the peanut and crushed it, the sound mingling in the furnished room with the big-city sounds coming through the open window—cars honking, feet on the sidewalk, children calling to each other, a plane overhead like a contented industrious bee.

"It is quite true," Mr. Crangle said at 3:49, "that only someone above all personal emotions, only someone who can look at the whole thing as if from the outside, can be trusted morally to make such a decision." As the big hand reached 3:50, he felt a sense of power surge deeply through him. "Think, Pet. In ten minutes. In ten little minutes, when I say the word, all the evil people all over the world will become half their present size, so they can be known. All the uncaught murderers and the tyrants and the proud and the sinful, all the bullies and the wrongdoers and the blackmailers and the nicotine fiends and the transgressors." His eyes blazed with omnipotence. "All of them, every one."

Pet said, "Nut."

Mr. Crangle gave her one.

"I know you don't agree fully with the half-size solution," he said, "but I do believe it to be the best one, all things considered."

He had studied the alternatives day and night since that morning three weeks ago when, as he sat on a bench in the park, looking at the pictures in the clouds across the lake, it came to him that he had the power to do this thing, that upon him at that moment had been bestowed the gift of putting a mark on all the bad people on earth, so that they should be known.

The realization surprised him not at all. Once before, such a thing happened. He had once held the power to stop wars. That was when the radio was telling about the big air raids on the cities. In that case the particular thing he could do was to take the stiffness out of airplane propellers, so that some morning when the crews, bundled like children against the cold, went out to get in their planes, they would find the props hanging limp, like empty banana skins.

That time he had delayed too long, waiting for just the right time and just the right plan, and they had outwitted him, unfairly. They had invented the jet, to which his power did not apply.

Then, too, there had been the thing about wheels. The thing about wheels came to him in a coffee place as he was looking at a newspaper photograph of a bad traffic accident, three killed. The power, that was, to change all the wheels in the world from round to square, or even to triangular if he wished, so they would stub in the asphalt and stop. But he wasn't allowed to keep that power. Before he could work out a plan and a time, he had felt it taken from him.

The power over bad people had stayed. It had even grown stronger, if power like that could grow stronger. And this time he had hurried, though of course there were certain problems to be thought through.

First, who was to decide what people were evil? That wasn't too hard, really, in spite of Pet's doubts. An evil person was a person who would seem evil to a man who held within himself the knowledge of good and evil, if that man could know all the person's innermost secrets. An evil person was a person who would seem evil to an all-knowing Mr. Crangle.

Then, how to do it, the method? Mark them on the forehead, or turn them all one color, say purple? But then they would simply be able to recognize each other the more readily and to band together in their wickedness.

When at last he hit upon the idea of a change of size, what came to him first was the thought of doubling the height and bulk of all the bad people. That would make them inefficient. They couldn't handle delicate scientific instruments or typewriters or adding machines or telephone dials. In time they would expire from bigness, like the dinosaurs in the article in the Sunday paper. But they might first run wild, with their great weight and strength, and hurt other people. Mr. Crangle wouldn't have liked that. He hated violence.

Half-size people, it was true, might be able to manipulate some of the machines. They could also be dangerous. But it would take them a long time to develop tools and weapons to their scale, and think how ridiculous they would be, meanwhile, with their clothes twice too big and their hats falling down over their ears.

At 3:54, Mr. Crangle smiled at the thought of how ridiculous they would be.

"Nut," Pet said.

He reached up and gave her one, his eyes still on the clock.

"I think," he said, "that the most interesting

place to be would be at a murder trial where nobody knew whether the accused was guilty or not. And then at 4 o'clock, if he was guilty—"

Mr. Crangle's breath was coming faster. The clock hands stood at 3:56.

"Or watching the drunkards in a saloon," he said.

"Nut," Pet said, and he gave her one.

He sat tense in his chair. He could actually see the big hand of the clock move, in the tiniest little jerkings, leaving a hairline of white between itself and the black 3:57 dot, and moving to the 3:58 dot, narrowing the space, until it touched that dot, and then stood directly on it, and then moved past toward the 3:59 dot.

"At first," Mr. Crangle said, "the newspapers won't believe it. Even though some of it will happen right in the newspaper offices, they won't believe it. At first they won't. And then when they begin to understand that it has happened to a lot of people everybody knows are evil, then they'll see the design."

The clock said 3:59.

"A great story," Mr. Crangle said. "A great newspaper story. And nobody will know who did it, Pet, nobody but you and me."

The point of the big hand crept halfway past the 3:59 dot. Mr. Crangle's heart beat hard. His eyes were wide, his lips parted. He whispered, "Nobody will know."

The tip of the big hand touched the dot at the top of the clock face. The alarm went off. Mr. Crangle felt a great surge of strength, like water bursting a dam, and a great shock, as of a bolt of lightning. He closed his eyes and took a deep breath.

"Now!" he said softly, and slumped exhausted.

By going to the window and looking down at the crowd in the street, he could have seen whether it had worked or not. He did not go to the window. He did not need to. He knew.

The alarm bell ran down.

Pet cocked her head and looked at him with an eye like polished stone.

"Nut," she said.

His hand, as he stretched it up, failed by a full foot and a half to reach the cage.

AUGUST HEAT
W. F. HARVEY

PHENISTONE ROAD, CLAPHAM, AUGUST 20, 1900—
I have had what I believe to be the most remarkable day in my life, and while the events
are still fresh in my mind, I wish to put them
down on paper as clearly as possible.

Let me say at the outset that my name is
James Clarence Withencroft. I am forty years
old, in perfect health, never having known a
day's illness.

By profession I am an artist, not a very suc-
cessful one, but I earn enough money by my
black-and-white work to satisfy my necessary
wants.

My only near relative, a sister, died five years
ago, so that I am independent.

I breakfasted this morning at nine. After glancing through the morning paper I lighted my pipe

and proceeded to let my mind wander in the hope that I might chance upon some subject for my pencil.

The room, though door and windows were open, was oppressively hot, and I had just made up my mind that the coolest and most comfortable place in the neighborhood would be the deep end of the public swimming bath, when the idea came.

I began to draw. So intent was I on my work that I left my lunch untouched, only stopping when the clock of St. Jude's struck four.

The final result, for a hurried sketch, was, I felt sure, the best thing I had done.

It showed a criminal in the dock immediately after the judge had pronounced sentence. The man was fat—enormously fat. The flesh hung in rolls about his chin; it creased his huge, stumpy neck. He was clean-shaven (perhaps I should say a few days before he must have been clean-shaven) and almost bald. He stood in the dock, his short, clumsy fingers clasping the rail, looking straight in front of him. The feeling that his expression conveyed was not so much one of horror as of utter, absolute collapse.

I rolled up the sketch, and without quite knowing why, placed it in my pocket. Then, with the rare sense of happiness which the knowledge of a good thing well done gives, I left the house.

From there onward I have only the vaguest recollections of where I went. The one thing of which I was fully conscious was the awful heat that came up from the dusty asphalt pavement as an almost palpable wave. I longed for the thunder promised by the great banks of copper-colored cloud that hung low over the western sky.

I must have walked five or six miles, when a small boy roused me from my reverie by asking the time.

It was twenty minutes to seven.

When he left me I began to take stock of my bearings. I found myself standing before a gate that led into a yard bordered by a strip of thirsty earth, where there were flowers—purple stock and scarlet geranium. Above the entrance was a board with the inscription—

CHS. ATKINSON   MONUMENTAL MASON
WORKER IN ENGLISH AND ITALIAN MARBLES

From the yard itself came a cheery whistle, the noise of hammer blows, and the cold sound of steel meeting stone.

A sudden impulse made me enter.

A man was sitting with his back toward me, busy at work on a slab of curiously veined marble. He turned round as he heard my steps and stopped short.

It was the man whose portrait lay in my pocket.

He sat there, huge and elephantine, the sweat pouring from his scalp, which he wiped with a red silk handkerchief. But though the face was the same, the expression was absolutely different.

He greeted me smiling, as if we were old friends. I apologized for my intrusion.

"Everything is hot and glary outside," I said. "This seems an oasis in the wilderness."

"I don't know about the oasis," he replied, "but

it certainly is hot, as hot as hell. Take a seat, sir!"

He pointed to the end of the gravestone on which he was at work, and I sat down.

"That's a beautiful piece of stone you've got hold of," I said.

He shook his head. "In a way it is," he answered; "the surface here is as fine as anything you could wish, but there's a big flaw at the back, though I don't expect you'd ever notice it. I could never make a really good job of a bit of marble like that. It would be all right in the summer like this; it wouldn't mind the blasted heat. But wait till the winter comes. There's nothing quite like frost to find out the weak points in stone."

"Then what's it for?" I asked.

The man burst out laughing.

"You'd hardly believe me if I was to tell you it's for an exhibition, but it's the truth. Artists have exhibitions; so do grocers and butchers; we have them too. All the latest little things in headstones, you know."

He went on to talk of marbles, which sort best withstood wind and rain, and which were easiest to work; then of his garden and a new sort of carnation he had bought. At the end of every other minute he would drop his tools, wipe his shining head, and curse the heat.

I said little, for I felt uneasy. There was something unnatural, uncanny, in meeting this man.

I tried at first to persuade myself that I had seen him before, that his face, unknown to me, had found a place in some out-of-the-way corner of my memory, but I knew that I was practicing

little more than a plausible piece of self-decep-
tion.

Mt. Atkinson finished his work, spat on the
ground, but got up with a sigh of relief.

"There! What do you think of that?" he said,
with pride.

The inscription which I read for the first time
was this—

SACRED TO THE MEMORY OF
JAMES CLARENCE WITHENCROFT
BORN JAN. 18TH, 1860
HE PASSED AWAY VERY SUDDENLY
ON AUGUST 20TH, 1900
"In the midst of life we are in death."

For some time I sat in silence. Then a cold
shudder ran down my spine. I asked him where
he had seen the name.

"Oh, I didn't see it anywhere," replied Mr.
Atkinson. "I wanted some name, and I put down
the first that came into my head. Why do you
want to know?"

"It's a strange coincidence, but it happens to
be mine."

He gave a long, low whistle. "And the dates?"

"I can only answer for one of them, and that's
correct."

"It's a rum go!" he said.

But he knew less than I did. I told him of
my morning's work. I took the sketch from my
pocket and showed it to him. As he looked, the
expression of his face altered until it became
more and more like that of the man I had
drawn.

"And it was only the day before yesterday," he said, "that I told Maria that there were no such things as ghosts!"

Neither of us had seen a ghost, but I knew what he meant. "You probably heard my name," I said.

"And you must have seen me somewhere and have forgotten it. Were you at Clacton-on-Sea last July?"

I had never been to Clacton in my life. We were silent for some time. We were both looking at the same thing, the two dates on the gravestone, and one was right.

"Come inside and have some supper," said Mr. Atkinson.

His wife is a cheerful little woman, with the flaky red cheeks of the country-bred. Her husband introduced me as a friend of his who was an artist. The result was unfortunate, for after the sardines and watercress had been removed, she brought me out a Doré Bible, and I had to sit and express my admiration for half an hour.

I went outside, and found Atkinson sitting on the gravestone smoking.

We resumed conversation where we had left off.

"Excuse my asking," I said, "but do you know of anything you've done for which you could be put on trial?"

He shook his head.

"I'm not a bankrupt, the business is prosperous enough. Three years ago I gave turkeys to some of the guardians at Christmas, but that's all I can think of. And they were small ones, too," he added as an afterthought.

He got up, fetched a can from the porch, and began to water the flowers. "Twice a day regular in the hot weather," he said, "and then the heat sometimes gets the better of the delicate ones. Where do you live?"

I told him my address. It would take an hour's quick walk to get back home.

"It's like this," he said. "We'll look at the matter straight. If you go back tonight, you take your chance of accidents. A cart may run over you, and there's always banana skins and orange peel, to say nothing of fallen ladders."

He spoke of the improbable with an intense seriousness that would have been laughable six hours before.

"The best thing we can do," he continued, "is for you to stay here till twelve o'clock. We'll go upstairs and smoke; it may be cooler inside."

To my surprise, I agreed.

We are sitting in a long, low room beneath the eaves. Atkinson has sent his wife to bed. He himself is busy sharpening some tools at a little oil stone, smoking.

The air seems charged with thunder. I am writing this at a shaky table before the open window. The leg is cracked, and Atkinson, who seems a handy man with his tools, is going to mend it as soon as he has finished putting an edge on his chisel.

It is after eleven now. I shall be gone in less than an hour.

But the heat is stifling. It is enough to send a man mad.

THE VERTICAL LADDER

WILLIAM SANSOM

As HE FELT the first watery eggs of sweat moistening the palms of his hands, as with every rung higher his body seemed to weigh more heavily, this young man Flegg regretted, in sudden desperation but still in vain, the irresponsible events that had thrust him up into his present precarious climb. Here he was, isolated on a vertical iron ladder flat to the side of a gasometer—a huge storage tank—and bound to climb higher and higher until he should reach the vertiginous skyward summit.

How could he ever have wished this on himself? How easy it had been to laugh away his cautionary fears on the firm ground. . . . Now he would give the very hands that clung to the ladder for a safe conduct to solid earth.

It had been a strong spring day, abruptly as

warm as midsummer. The sun flooded the park streets with sudden heat and Flegg and his friends had felt stifled in their thick winter clothes. The green glare of the new leaves everywhere struck the eye too fiercely, and the air seemed almost sticky from the exhalations of buds and swelling resins. Cold winter senses were overcome—the girls had complained of headaches—and their thoughts had grown confused and uncomfortable as the wool underneath against their skins. They had wandered out from the park by a back gate, into an area of back streets.

The houses there were small and old, some of them already falling into disrepair; short streets, cobbles, narrow pavements, and the only shops a tobacconist or a desolate corner oil shop to color the gray—it was the outcrop of some industrial undertaking beyond. At first these quiet, almost deserted streets had seemed more restful than the park; but soon a dusty air of peeling plaster and powdering brick, the dark windows and the dry stone steps, the very dryness altogether had proved more wearying than before, so that when suddenly the houses ended and the ground opened to reveal the yards of a disused gasworks, Flegg and his friends had welcomed the green of nettles and milkwort that grew among the scrap iron and broken brick.

They walked out into the wasteland, the two girls and Flegg and the other two boys, and stood presently before the old gasometer itself. Among the ruined sheds this was the only erection still whole; it still predominated over the yards, towering high above other buildings for hundreds of feet around. So they threw bricks against its rusted sides.

The rust flew off in flakes and the iron rang dully. Flegg, who wished to excel in the eyes of the dark-haired girl, began throwing his bricks higher than the others, at the same time lobbing them, to suggest that he knew something of grenade throwing, claiming vicariously the glamour of a uniform. He felt the girl's eyes follow his shoulders, and his shoulders broadened. She had black eyes, unshadowed beneath short wide-awake lids; her lips pouted with difficulty over a scramble of irregular teeth, so that it often looked as if she were laughing; she always frowned—and Flegg liked her earnest, purposeful expression. Altogether she seemed a wide-awake girl who would be the first to appreciate an active sort of a man. Now she frowned and shouted: "Bet you can't climb as high as you can throw!"

Then there began one of those uneasy jokes, innocent at first, that taken seriously can accumulate a hysterical accumulation of spite. Everyone recognizes this underlying unpleasantness, it is plainly felt, but just because of this the joke must at all costs be pressed forward; one becomes frightened, one laughs all the louder, pressing to drown the embarrassments of danger and guilt. The third boy had instantly shouted: "Course he can't, he can't climb no higher than himself."

Flegg turned round scoffing, so that the girl had quickly shouted again, laughing shrilly and pointing upward. Already all five of them felt uneasy. Then in quick succession, all in a few seconds, the third boy had repeated: "Course he bloody can't." Flegg had said: "Climb to the top of anything." The other boy had said, "Climb to the top of my Aunt Fanny." The girl had said: "Climb to the top of the gasworks then."

Flegg had said: "That's nothing." And the girl, pressing on then as she had to, suddenly introduced the inevitable detail that made these suppositions into fact: "Go on then, climb it. Here —tie my hanky on the top. Tie my flag to the top."

Even then Flegg had a second's chance. It occurred to him instantly that he could laugh it off; but a hysterical emphasis now possessed the girl's face—she was dancing up and down and clapping her hands insistently—and this confused Flegg. He began stuttering after the right words. But the words refused to come. At all costs he had to cover his stuttering. So: "Off we go then!" he had said. And he had turned to the gasometer.

It was not, after all, so very high. It was hardly a full-sized gasometer, its trellised iron toprail would have stood level with the roof-coping of a five- or six-story tenement. Until then Flegg had only seen the gasometer as a rough mass of iron, but now every detail sprang into abrupt definition. He studied it intently, alertly considering its size and every feature of stability—the brown rusted iron sheeting smeared here and there with red lead, a curious buckling that sometimes deflated its curved bulk as though a vacuum were collapsing it from within,

the ladders scaling the sides, flush with the sheeting, the grid of girders, a complexity of struts,
the bolting.

There were two ladders, one a Jacob's ladder,
clamped fast to the side, another that was more
of a staircase, zigzagging up the belly of the
gasometer in easy gradients and provided with a
safety rail. This must have been erected later as
a substitute for the Jacob's ladder, which demanded an unnecessarily stringent climb and
was now in disuse, for some twenty feet of its
longer rungs had been worn away; however,
there was apparently some painting in progress,
for a painter's wooden ladder had been propped
beneath, reaching to the undamaged bottom of
the vertical ladder—the ascent was thus service-
able again. Flegg looked quickly at the foot of
the wooden ladder—was it well grounded?—and
then at the head farther up—was this secure?—
and then up to the top, screwing his eyes to
note any fault in the iron rungs reaching in-
numerably, indistinctly, and dizzyingly to the
summit platform.

Flegg, rapidly assessing these structures, never
stopped sauntering forward. He was committed,
and so while deliberately sauntering to appear
thus the more at ease, he knew that he must
never hesitate. The two boys and his own girl
kept up a chorus of encouraging abuse. "How I
Climbed Mount Everest," they shouted. "He'll
come down quicker'n he went up." "Mind you
don't bang your head on a harp, Sir Galahad."
But the second girl had remained quiet throughout; she was already frightened, sensing in-

stantly that the guilt for some tragedy was hers alone—although she had never in fact opened her mouth. Now she chewed passionately on gum.

Suddenly the chorus rose shriller. Flegg had veered slightly toward the safer staircase. His eyes had naturally questioned this along with the rest of the gasometer, and almost unconsciously his footsteps had veered in the direction of his eyes. Then his instinct had emerged into full consciousness—perhaps he could use the staircase; no one had actually instanced the Jacob's ladder; there might yet be a chance? But the quick eyes behind him had seen, and immediately the chorus rose: "No, you don't!" "Not up those sissy stairs!" Flegg switched his course by only the fraction that turned him again to the perpendicular ladder. "Who's talking about stairs?" he shouted back.

Behind him they still kept up a din, still kept him up to pitch, worrying at him viciously. "Look at him, he doesn't know which way to go —he's like a ruddy duck's uncle without an aunt." So that Flegg realized finally that there was no alternative. He had to climb the gasometer by the vertical ladder. And as soon as this was finally settled, the doubt cleared from his mind. He braced his shoulders and suddenly found himself really making light of the job. After all, he thought, it isn't so high. Why should I worry? Hundreds of men climb such ladders each day, no one falls, the ladders are clamped as safe as houses. He began to smile within himself at his earlier perturbations. Added to this, the girl now ran up to him and handed him her handkerchief. As her black eyes frowned a smile at him, he saw that her expression no longer held its vicious, laughing scorn, but now instead had grown softer, with a look of real encouragement and even admiration. "Here's your flag," she said. And then she even added: "Tell you what—you don't really have to go! I'll believe you!" But this came too late. Flegg had accepted the climb, it was fact, and already he felt something of an exhilarating glow of glory. He took the handkerchief, blew the girl a dramatic kiss, and started up the lowest rungs of the ladder at a run.

This painter's ladder was placed at a comfortable slant. But nevertheless Flegg had only climbed some ten feet—what might have corresponded to the top of a first floor window—when he began to slow up; he stopped running and gripped harder at the rungs above and placed his feet more firmly on the unseen bars below. Although he had not yet measured his distance from the ground, somehow he sensed he was already unnaturally high, with nothing but air and a precarious skeleton of wooden bars between him and the receding ground. He felt independent of solid support; yet, according to his eyes, which stared straight forward at the iron sheeting beyond, he might have been standing on the lowest rungs by the ground. The sensation of height infected him strongly; it had become an urgent necessity to maintain a balance; each muscle of his body became unnaturally alert. This was not an unpleasant feeling; he almost enjoyed a new athletic command of every precarious movement. He climbed methodically until he reached the ladder head and the first of the perpendicular iron rungs.

Here for a moment Flegg had paused. He had rested his knees up against the last three steps of the safely slanting wooden ladder. He had grasped the two side supports of the rusted iron that led so straightly upward. His knees then clung to the motherly wood; his hands felt the iron cold and gritty. The rust powdered off and smeared him with its red dust; one large scrap flaked off and fell on his face as he looked upward. He wanted to brush this away from his eye, but the impulse was, to his surprise, much less powerful than the viselike will that clutched his hands to the iron support. His hands remained firmly gripping the iron; he had to shake off the rust flake with a jerk of his head. Even then this sharp movement nearly unbalanced him, and his stomach gulped coldly with sudden shock. He settled his knees more firmly against the wood, and though he forced himself to laugh at his sudden feat, so that in some measure his poise did really return, nevertheless he did not alter the awkward knock-kneed position of his legs patently clinging for safety. With all this he had scarcely paused. Now he pulled at the stanchions of the iron ladder; they were as firm as if they had been driven into rock.

He looked up, following the dizzying rise of the rungs to the skyline. From this angle flat against the iron sheeting, the gasometer appeared higher than before. The blue sky seemed to descend and almost touch it. The redness of the rust dissolved into a deepening gray shadow; the distant curved summit loomed over black and high. Although it was immensely stable, as seen in rounded perspective from a few yards away, there against the side it appeared top-heavy, so that this huge segment of sheet iron seemed to have lost the support of its invisible complement behind, the support that was now unseen and therefore unfelt, and Flegg imagined despite himself that the entire erection had become unsteady, that quite possibly the gasometer might suddenly blow over like a gigantic top-heavy sail. He lowered his eyes quickly and concentrated on the hands before him. He began to climb.

From beneath there still rose a few cries from the boys. But the girl had stopped shouting— probably she was following Flegg's every step with admiring eyes. He imagined again her frown and her peculiarly pouting mouth, and from this image drew new strength with which he clutched the rungs more eagerly. But now he noticed that the cries had begun to ring with an unpleasant new echo, as though they were already far off. And Flegg could not so easily distinguish their words. Even at this height he seemed to have penetrated into a distinct stratum of separate air, for it was certainly cooler, and for the first time that day he felt the light fanning of a wind. He looked down. His friends appeared shockingly small. Their bodies had disappeared and he saw only their upturned faces. He wanted to wave, to demonstrate in some way a carefree attitude; but then instantly he felt frustrated as his hands refused to unlock their grip. He turned to the rungs again with the smile dying on his lips.

He swallowed uneasily and continued to tread slowly upward, hand after hand, foot after foot. He had climbed ten rungs of the iron ladder when his hands first began to feel moist, when suddenly, as though a catastrophe had overtaken him, not gradually but in one overpowering second, he realized that he was afraid. Incontrovertibly. He could cover it no longer; he admitted it all over his body. His hands gripped with pitiable eagerness; they were now alert to a point of shivering, as though the nerves inside them had been forced taut for so long that now they had burst beyond their strained tegument; his feet no longer trod firmly on the rungs beneath but first stepped for their place timorously, then glued themselves to the iron. In this way his body lost most of its poise; these nerves and muscles in his two legs and two arms seemed to work independently, no longer integrated with the rhythm of his body, but moving with the dangerous unwilled jerk of crippled limbs.

His body hung slack away from the ladder, with nothing beneath it but a thirty-foot drop to the ground; only his hands and feet were fed with the security of an attachment; most of him lay off the ladder, hanging in space; his arms revolted at the strain of their familiar angle, as though they were flies' feet denying all natural laws. For the first time, as the fear took hold of him, he felt that what he had attempted was impossible. He could never achieve the top. If at this height of only thirty feet, as if it were three stories of a building, he felt afraid—what would he feel at sixty feet? Yet . . . he trod heavily up. He was afraid, but not desperate. He dreaded each stop, yet forced himself to believe that at some time it would be over; it could not take long.

A memory crossed his mind. It occurred to him vividly, then flashed away, for his eyes and mind were continually concentrated on the rusted iron bars and the white knuckles of his hands. But for an instant he remembered waking up long ago in the nursery and seeing that the windows were light, as if they reflected a coldness of moonlight. Only they were not so much lit by light as by a sensation of space. He had crawled out of bed and climbed onto a chair that stood beneath the window. It was as he had thought. Outside there was space, nothing else, a limited area of space; yet this was not unnatural, for soon his logical eyes had supplied, for what had at first appeared an impossible infinity, the later image of a perfectly reasonable flood. A vast plain of still water as far as his eyes could see. It lapped silently at the sides of the house, and in the light of an unseen moon winked and washed darkly, concealing great beasts of mystery beneath its black calm surface. This water attracted him; he wished to jump into it from the window and immerse himself in it and allow his head to sink slowly under. However, he was perched up too high. He felt, alone at the window, infinitely high, so that the flood seemed to lie in miniature at a great distance below, as later in life when he was ill he had seen the objects of his bedroom grow small and infinitely remote in the fevered reflection behind his eyes. Isolated at the little window, he had been frightened by the emptiness surrounding him—only the sky and the water and the marooned stone wall of the house; he had been terrified yet drawn down by dread and desire. Then a battleship had sailed by. He had wakened up, saved by the appearance of the battleship.

And now on the ladder he had a sudden hope that something as large and stable would intervene again to help him.

But ten rungs farther up he began to sweat more violently than ever. His hands streamed with red rust, and the flesh inside his thighs blenched. Another flake of rust fell on his forehead; this time it stuck in the wetness. He felt physically exhausted. Fear was draining his strength and the precarious position of his body. Each stressed muscle ached. His body weighed more heavily at each step upward; it sagged beneath his arms like a leaden sack. His legs no longer provided their adequate support; it seemed as though they needed every pull of their muscles to force themselves, as independent limbs, close to the ladder. The wind blew faster. It dragged now at his coat; it blew its space about him; it echoed silently a lonesome spaciousness. "Don't look down," the blood whispered in his temples; "Don't look down; DON'T LOOK DOWN."

Three quarters up the gasometer and fifty feet from the ground Flegg grew desperate. Every other consideration suddenly left him. He wanted only to reach ground as quickly as possible, only that. Nothing else mattered. He stopped climbing and clung to the ladder panting. Very slowly, lowering his eyes carefully so that he could raise them instantly if he saw too much, he looked down a rung, and another past his armpit, past his waist—and focused them on the ground beneath. He looked quickly up again.

He pressed himself to the ladder. Tears started in his eyes. For a moment they reeled red with giddiness. He closed them, shutting out everything. Then instantly he opened them, afraid that something might happen. He must watch his hands, watch the bars, watch the rusted iron sheeting itself; no movement should escape him; the struts might come creaking loose; the whole edifice might sway over; although a fading reason told him that the gasometer had remained firm for years and was still as steady as a cliff, his horrified senses suspected that this was the one moment in the building's life when a wind would blow that was too strong for it and some defective strut would snap and the whole edifice would heel over and crash to the ground. This image became so clear he could see the sheets of iron buckling and folding like cloth as the huge weight sank to the earth.

The ground had receded horribly; the drop now appeared terrifying, out of all proportion to this height he had reached. From the ground such a height would have appeared unnoteworthy. But now from here the distance seemed to have doubled. Each object familiar to his everyday eyes—his friends, the lampposts, a brick wall, the curb, a drain—all these had grown infinitely small. His senses demanded that these objects should be of a certain accustomed size. Alternately, the world of chimneys and attic windows and roof-coping would grow unpleasantly giant as his pavement-bred eyes approached. Even now the iron sheeting that stretched to either side and above and below seemed to have grown. He was lost among such huge smooth dimensions, grown smaller himself and clinging now like a child lost on some monstrous desert of red rust.

These unfamiliarities shocked his nerves more than the danger of falling. The sense of isolation was overpowering. All things were suddenly alien. Yet exposed on the iron spaces, with the unending winds blowing aerially round him, among such free things—he felt shut in! Trembling and panting so that he stifled himself with the shortness of his own breath, he took the first step downward. . . .

A commotion began below. A confusion of cries came drifting up to him. Above all he could hear the single voice of the girl who had so far kept quiet. She was screaming high, a shrill scream that rose in the air incisively like a gull's shriek. "Put it back, put it back, put it back!" the scream seemed to say. So that Flegg, thinking that these cries were to warn him of some new danger apparent only from the ground,

—Flegg gripped himself into the ladder and looked down again. He glanced down for a fractional second—but in that time saw enough. He saw that the girl was screaming and pointing to the base of the iron ladder. He saw the others crowding round her, gesticulating. He saw that she really had been crying, "Put it back!" And he realized now what the words meant—someone had removed the painter's ladder.

It lay clearly on the ground, outlined white like a child's drawing of a ladder. The boys must have seen his first step downward, and then, from fun or from spite, they had removed his only means of retreat. He remembered that from the base of the ladder to the ground the drop fell twenty feet. He considered quickly descending and appealing from the bottom of the ladder, but he foresaw that for precious minutes they would jeer and argue, refusing to replace the ladder, and he felt then that he could never risk these minutes, unnerved, with his strength failing. Besides, he had already noticed that the whole group of them were wandering off. The boys were driving the quiet girl away, now more concerned with her than with Flegg. The quiet girl's sense of guilt had been brought to a head by the removal of the ladder. Now she was hysterically terrified. She was yelling to them to put the ladder back. She—only she, the passive one—sensed the terror that awaited them all.

But her screams defeated their own purpose. They had altogether distracted the attention of the others; now it was fun to provoke more screams, to encourage this new distraction—and they forgot about Flegg far up and beyond them. They were wandering away. They were abandoning him, casually unconcerned that he was alone and helpless up in his wide prison of rust. His heart cried out for them to stay. He forgot their scorn in new and terrible torments of self-pity. An uneasy feeling lumped his throat; his eyes smarted with dry tears.

But they were wandering away. There was no retreat. They did not even know he was in difficulties. So Flegg had no option but to climb higher. Desperately he tried to shake off his fear; he actually shook his head. Then he stared hard at the rungs immediately facing his eyes and tried to imagine that he was not high up at all. He lifted himself tentatively by one rung, then by another, and in this way dragged himself higher and higher . . . until he must have been some ten rungs from the top, over the fifth story of a house, with now perhaps only one more story to climb. He imagined that he might then be approaching the summit platform, and to measure this last distance he looked up.

He looked up and heaved. He felt for the first time panicked beyond desperation, wildly violently loose. He almost let go. His senses screamed to let go, yet his hands refused to open. He was stretched on a rack made by these hands that would not unlock their grip and by the panic and desire to drop. The nerves left his hands so that they might have been dried bones of fingers gripped round the rungs, hooks of bone fixed perhaps strongly enough to cling on, or perhaps at some moment of pressure to uncurl their vertebrae and straighten to a drop. His insteps pricked with cold cramps. The sweat sickened him. His loins seemed to empty themselves. His trousers ran wet. He shivered, grew giddy, and flung himself froglike onto the ladder.

The sight of the top of the gasometer had proved endemically more frightful than the appearance of the drop beneath. There lay about it a sense of material danger, not of the risk of falling, but of something removed and unhuman —a sense of appalling isolation. It echoed its elemental iron aloofness; a wind blew round it that had never known the warmth of flesh nor the softness of green fibers. Its blind eyes were raised above the world. It was like the eyeless iron vizor of an ancient god. It touched against the sky having risen in awful perpendicular to this isolation, solitary as the gray gannet cliffs that marked the end of the northern world. It was immeasurably old, outside the connotation of time; it was nothing human, only washed by the high weather, echoing with wind, visited never, alone.

And in this summit Flegg measured clearly the full distance of his climb. This close skyline emphasized the whirling space beneath him. He clearly saw a man fall through this space, spread-eagling to smash with the sickening force of a locomotive on the stone beneath. The man turned slowly in the air, yet his thoughts raced faster than he fell.

Flegg, clutching his body close to the rust, made small weeping sounds through his mouth.

Shivering, shuddering, he began to tread up again, working his knees and elbows outward like a frog, so that with a hot roaring, he hurried himself, he began to scramble up wrenching at his last strength, whispering urgent meaningless words to himself like the swift whispers that close in on a nightmare. A huge weight pulled at him, dragging him to drop. He climbed higher. He reached the top rung—and found his face staring still at a wall of red rust. He looked, wild with terror. It was the top rung! The ladder had ended! Yet—no platform . . . the real top rungs were missing . . . the platform jutted five impassable feet above. . . . Flegg stared dumbly, encircling his head like a lost animal . . . then he jammed his legs in the lower rungs and his arms to the armpits in through the top rungs and there he hung shivering, past knowing what more he could ever do. . . .

THE SEA GULLS
ELIAS VENEZIS

THE LITTLE ISLAND off the north of Lesbos, between Petra and Molyvos, is barren and uninhabited. It has no name, and fishermen who work in those seas simply call it "the island." No trees grow on it, only a few shrubs. Three miles away the mountains of Lesbos compose a gentle harmony of line, movement, and color. In face of this prodigality, the bare islet with its severe outline seems still more of a desert. It is as if God had forgotten it when He made the sea and the dry land in the first seven days of the world.

But in the summer, from this bare strip of earth, you can see the sun set in the open sea. Then the waters take color and continually change every minute as if the light were melting in little waves. When it is a very clear evening, you can distinguish the mountains of Athos coming out of the sea, and then slowly disappearing in the falling dusk. At this hour old Dimitri, the sole inhabitant of the desert island, will perform the one action that unites him with life and his fellow men; he will light the lamp in the lighthouse. The light will begin to flare up and to flicker, again and again, in the same rhythm, gravely, inevitably—like the dark powers of life, like destiny, like death.

The old lighthouse keeper drew his boat up onto the sand.

"Well, that journey is over . . ." he said quietly. He spoke to himself, and then was silent. This crossing to the opposite shore took place once a month. He went for his provisions—flour, oil, and the few other things he needed. In earlier years when he made the crossing he used to stay the whole day in the village. He would talk to old friends, hear the local news and the news of the world, whether people were at peace or war.

The customs officer would pay him his wages. "Well, come back all right next month, Dimitri."

The old man would nod his head and thank him. "God willing, if we're alive, my son."

The rest of the time till he returned to "his island" he spent in going up to the little Chapel of Our Lady, on the rock with the hundred steps, to say his prayers. He would cross his arms in front of the old icon, bow his head, and pray for his two sons, lost in the Asia Minor disaster, for other people, and lastly for himself.

So it used to be every time, on every visit.

But as the years passed, he drew away from human contact. Solitude gradually mastered him, absorbed him, day by day, as if with its terrible power it was filtering into his very being. Now he would try to shorten the time he had to stay in the village for his business. He even gave up the climb to the chapel on the rock. "Forgive me, I can't climb any more," he would say to God, as if it were a sin. "I can pray to you anywhere, and you see how feeble I am."

And when he got back to his island, after every journey, he would stay up for a long time in prayer, under the stars. He no longer asked for news of what was going on in the world. He didn't want to know. Day by day the whole world tightened round the little island, closing it in with the deep sea and its colors, as the sun declined.

At last the only people he spoke to were fishermen, who put in to his island when bad weather overtook them. They stayed on the shore, waiting for the sea to calm, and talked about their troubles and their luck. They would spend the whole night there with the old man. Sometimes just before dawn, when other subjects were exhausted, he would speak of his two lost sons.

"Who knows?" said the fishermen. "Perhaps they're alive and will come back, Dimitri. Just like your sea gulls."

He did not speak or move; his eyes stared into the night.

"Yes, Dimitri, like your sea gulls. Your boys may come back as they did. Don't give up hope." Then they would talk about the old man's sea gulls.

"Is it true, Dimitri, that you managed to tame them? Nobody ever heard of sea gulls being tame. . . ."

"Yes, they were tame. Everything here below can be tamed—except man."

They asked him to tell them the story of the sea gulls again, though they knew it, as everyone did who lived on the opposite shore. He had found them among the rocks, two tiny sea gulls, still unfledged. It was winter, and he took them to his cottage beside the lighthouse. He kept them and brought them up, feeding them on the minnows from his net. One day he thought of giving them names.

"Well, you, we'll call you . . ." That day his heart and memory were full of his two children —at the time when they were very young, and he used to shout after them. "We'll . . . we'll call you Vasilaki," he said to one bird. "And let's call you Argyri." So from then on he began to call them by his sons' names, and in time the sea gulls almost seemed to recognize them.

When the birds were grown—it was almost spring—he thought one morning that it was a shame to keep them in captivity. He decided to set them free. He opened the big wicker cage and took out one bird. He held it in his hands and stroked it. He felt his heart lighten.

"Well, good-bye, Vasilaki!" he said to the bird, and opened his hands to let it fly. The gull flew away. He took out the other, stroking it as he had the first, and let it go too. Everything was peaceful that day, and the night that followed was quiet. Only he felt still more alone.

That evening—he had gone to bed early—he heard light tappings on the cottage window. He went to look . . . and could hardly believe it. He was overcome with joy, as if it were his sons returning. He opened the door for the gulls to fly in.

And from then on this is what happened: the birds would fly off in the morning, voyage as far as the Asiatic mainland, or to Sigri, but they always came back in the evening. They would join in flocks of other gulls, and often flew over the island. If they flew low, the old man would recognize them by the ash-colored markings under their wings. When he went out in his boat, and they were circling near, the gulls would fly low and screech around him. The other fishermen got to know them, and when they saw them they laughed, and shouted: "Vasilaki! Argyri!"

So the days went by on the desert island—one like another—an uninterrupted series of days and nights leading to nothing, except to death. But one summer evening something unusual happened. The gulls did not return. Nor did they come back next day, nor the following night. "Perhaps they made a very long journey," the old man told himself, trying to cheat his anxiety.

Next morning he was sitting on the stone parapet of the lighthouse, looking out to sea. About a mile offshore the sea was being furrowed as if dolphins were playing there. He liked to watch for dolphins passing, following their slow movements as they rose like silver out of the water and slipped back into it again.

"It must be dolphins again." But soon he saw clearly that it was not. "They're people!" he cried in astonishment.

He went down to the shore to wait. Soon he saw clearly that it was a boy and a girl. They were swimming side by side, with slow strokes, full of confidence. And the little waves closed over the furrow they drew behind them. What could they be doing? He did not remember people swimming there ever before. Nor did there seem to be any boat from which they could have fallen.

Soon they reached the shore. The two wet young people stood on the beach, shaking the sea off themselves. The boy looked the girl in the eye, stretched his arms above his head, drew a deep breath, and said: "Ah! That was fine!" The girl made the same motion with her arms more slowly: "It was fine!" Then they ran toward the lighthouse keeper.

"You're Uncle Dimitri?" asked the boy.

The old man stood up. "Yes, I am," he said, in confusion. "Have you had an accident?"

"Oh, no!" said the boy quickly. "Yesterday my friend and I were saying we should try to swim out here . . . and here we are!"

"Where have you come from?" asked the old man in astonishment.

"Why, from Petra, over there."

Dimitri did not know what to say, and could only murmur that he never remembered anyone's getting to the island without a boat before. He invited them to come up to the lighthouse and

he led the way, with the young people following. They could neither of them be more than
eighteen or nineteen. The old man went in front,
and his years as he climbed seemed to weigh on
him more heavily than usual as if reproachful
because he would not let them rest.

They sat on the parapet of the lighthouse—
below them the waveless Aegean and the sun
trembling above it.

"Where do you come from?" asked the old
man.

"We're students in Athens," said the girl. "I
study chemistry, and he's at the Polytechnic."

"Oh, really! . . ." murmured the old man,
without understanding.

"Have you ever been to Athens?" asked the
girl.

"No, never."

"Would you like to go?"

His voice was soft, could scarcely be heard:
"No, child, it's too late now."

"You must be very much alone here."

"Yes, I'm very much alone, my child."

They were silent. A short time passed. A flight
of gulls went by, high up in the sky. The old
man got up and went into the cottage to find
something to offer them. From the little window
he could see the two young people, where they
had stretched out on the parapet. Drops of
water from the sea still trembled on their bodies
and their faces. The sun had tanned them deeply,
and they lay there like two bronze statues cast
up by the sea—a god of youth and a goddess of
health. The girl's black hair fell over her shoul-

ders, and a deep light moved in her large dark eyes. The boy lifted himself and bent toward her, drawn to her as if in a dream. Gently his fingers touched her cheek.

"Hrysoula . . ." he only murmured her name, his lips trembling with emotion. The dark eyes were lifted and remained motionless for a moment, fixed on the boy's face. Then she clasped her hands about his head and kissed him passionately.

Everything was simple and quiet on the desert island in that blessed moment, and all was quiet in the old man's heart. He was filled with happiness that summer morning, his eyes brimming with tears. This unforeseen tenderness that had entered his solitude, and the motionless sea. . .

"Grandpa, shall we come in too?" the girl called.

"I'm coming, I'm coming," he said in confusion.

He brought them fruit, almonds, and cold water. "I've nothing else . . ." he murmured, as if asking their pardon.

"Sit down, sit down, Grandpa." The girl took him by the hand and made him sit down by her.

"Come back tomorrow," he said timidly. "I'll catch some fish for you tonight."

"We have to go home tomorrow," said the girl. "What a pity we were here all these days without coming over! Are you always alone like this, Grandpa?"

"Always, my child."

"Ah, now I understand about the gulls," said the boy.

"Yes, my son, that's what it is. Solitude."

"You must forgive them, Grandpa," the boy said. "If they'd known, they would never have done it."

The old man did not understand. He paused, bewildered. "Who are you talking about, my son?"

"The people who killed your sea gulls, I mean. They were old friends of ours."

The old man felt his knees trembling. "Did you say . . . they killed them?"

"Didn't you know? . . ." The boy bit his lip, but it was too late. He told him the story. They had gone out shooting, all the young people, down by the shore; the two gulls flew lower than the others, and their friend brought them down. Later some fishermen had recognized the ash-colored markings on their wings.

The old man listened silently. It was nothing, only two sea gulls.

"They didn't know, Grandpa . . ." said the girl gently, moved by the dumb grief which she saw on the old face. "They didn't know."

He nodded his head slowly in assent. "Yes, my child. They couldn't have known. . . ."

Some time went by. "We must go," said the boy. The girl got up. "Yes, we must start back." They went ahead, the old man following a little behind them.

"Good-bye, Grandpa," said the girl. She took his hand and bent to kiss it. He stroked her long hair. "God bless you," he murmured with emotion.

They waded into the sea and swam off. For a

long time he watched the little furrow their bodies drew in the sea. Then they faded from his sight, and the sea was empty.

Night fell. He sat on the parapet of the lighthouse, and the hours went by. Everything passed before his dim eyes; his youth, the sons he had brought up and lost, and the people who had hurt him. All passed, all faded—even the two young people who had kissed each other on that very spot a few hours before. And a flight of gulls flying high, two with ash-colored wings. They were gone too. Nothing remained that would come back.

His head sank forward and his tears fell on the dry earth. Above him the lighthouse lamp flickered, again and again, in the same rhythm, slowly, inevitably, like the dark powers of life, like destiny, like death.

ANTAEUS
BORDEN DEAL

THIS WAS DURING THE WARTIME, when lots of people were coming north for jobs in factories and war industries, when people moved around a lot more than they do now and sometimes kids were thrown into new groups and new lives that were completely different from anything they had ever known before. I remember this one kid; T. J. his name was, from somewhere down South, whose family moved into our building during that time. They'd come north with everything they owned piled into the back seat of an old model sedan that you wouldn't expect could make the trip, with T. J. and his three younger sisters riding shakily atop the load of junk.

Our building was just like all the others there, with families crowded into a few rooms, and I guess there were twenty-five or thirty kids about my age in that one building. Of course, there were a few of us who formed a gang and ran together all the time after school, and I was the one who brought T. J. in and started the whole thing.

The building right next door to us was a factory where they made walking dolls. It was a low building with a flat, tarred roof that had a parapet all around it about head-high and we'd found out a long time before that no one, not even the watchman, paid any attention to the roof because it was higher than any of the other buildings around. So my gang used the roof as a headquarters. We could get up there by crossing over to the fire escape from our own roof on a plank and then going on up. It was a secret place for us, where nobody else could go without our permission.

I remember the day I first took T. J. up there to meet the gang. He was a stocky, robust kid with a shock of white hair, nothing sissy about him except his voice—he talked different from any of us and you noticed it right away. But I liked him anyway, so I told him to come on up.

We climbed up over the parapet and dropped down on the roof. The rest of the gang were already there.

"Hi," I said. I jerked my thumb at T. J. "He just moved into the building yesterday."

He just stood there, not scared or anything, just looking, like the first time you see somebody you're not sure you're going to like.

"Hi," Blackie said. "Where you from?"

"Marion County," T. J. said.

We laughed. "Marion County?" I said. "Where's that?"

He looked at me like I was a stranger too. "It's in Alabama," he said, like I ought to know where it was.

"What's your name?" Charley said.

"T. J.," he said, looking back at him. He had pale blue eyes that looked washed-out but he looked directly at Charley, waiting for his reaction. He'll be all right, I thought. No sissy in him . . . except that voice. Who ever talked like that?

"T. J.," Blackie said. "That's just initials. What's your real name? Nobody in the world has just initials."

"I do," he said. "And they're T. J. That's all the name I got."

His voice was resolute with the knowledge of his rightness and for a moment no one had anything to say. T. J. looked around at the rooftop and down at the black tar under his feet. "Down yonder where I come from," he said, "we played out in the woods. Don't you-all have no woods around here?"

"Naw," Blackie said. "There's a park a few blocks over, but it's full of kids and cops and old women. You can't do a thing."

T. J. kept looking at the tar under his feet. "You mean you ain't got no fields to raise nothing in? No watermelons or nothing?"

"Naw," I said scornfully. "What do you want to grow something for? The folks can buy everything they need at the store."

He looked at me again with that strange, unknowing look. "In Marion County," he said, "I had my own acre of cotton and my own acre of corn. It was mine to plant ever' year."

He sounded like it was something to be proud of, and in some obscure way it made the rest of us angry. "Heck!" Blackie said. "Who'd want to have their own acre of cotton and corn? That's just work. What can you do with an acre of cotton and corn?"

T. J. looked at him. "Well, you get part of the bale offen your acre," he said seriously. "And I fed my acre of corn to my calf."

We didn't really know what he was talking about, so we were more puzzled than angry; otherwise, I guess, we'd have chased him off the roof and wouldn't let him be part of our gang. But he was strange and different and we were all attracted by his stolid sense of rightness and belonging, maybe by the strange softness of his voice contrasting our own tones of speech into harshness.

He moved his foot against the black tar. "We could make our own field right here," he said softly, thoughtfully. "Come spring we could raise us what we want to . . . watermelons and garden truck and no telling what all."

"You'd have to be a good farmer to make these tar roofs grow any watermelons," I said. We all laughed.

But T. J. looked serious. "We could haul us some dirt up here," he said. "And spread it out even and water it and before you know it we'd have us a crop in here." He looked at us intently. "Wouldn't that be fun?"

"They wouldn't let us," Blackie said quickly.

"I thought you said this was you-all's roof," T. J. said to me. "That you-all could do anything you wanted up here."

"They've never bothered us," I said. I felt the idea beginning to catch fire in me. It was a big idea and it took a while for it to sink in but the more I thought about it the better I liked it. "Say," I said to the gang, "he might have something there. Just make us a regular roof garden, with flowers and grass and trees and everything. And all ours," I said. "We wouldn't let anybody up here except the ones we wanted to."

"It'd take a while to grow trees," T. J. said quickly, but we weren't paying any attention to him. They were all talking about it suddenly, all excited with the idea after I'd put it in a way they could catch hold of it. Only rich people had roof gardens, we knew, and the idea of our own private domain excited them.

"We could bring it up in sacks and boxes," Blackie said. "We'd have to do it while the folks weren't paying any attention to us. We'd have to come up to the roof of our building and then cross over with it."

"Where could we get the dirt?" someone said worriedly.

"Out of those vacant lots over close to school," Blackie said. "Nobody'd notice if we scraped it up."

I slapped T. J. on the shoulder. "Man, you had a wonderful idea," I said, and everybody grinned at him, remembering he had started it. "Our own private roof garden."

He grinned back. "It'll be ourn," he said. "All ourn." Then he looked thoughtful again. "Maybe I can lay my hands on some cotton seed too. You think we could raise us some cotton?"

We'd started big projects before at one time or another, like any gang of kids, but they'd always petered out for lack of organization and direction. But this one didn't. . . . Somehow or other T. J. kept it going all through the winter months. He kept talking about the watermelons and the cotton we'd raise, come spring, and when even that wouldn't work he'd switch around to my idea of flowers and grass and trees though he was always honest enough to add that it'd take a while to get any trees started. He always had it on his mind and he'd mention it in school, getting them lined up to carry dirt that afternoon, saying in a casual way that he reckoned a few more weeks ought to see the job through.

Our little area of private earth grew slowly. T. J. was smart enough to start in one corner of the building, heaping up the carried earth two or three feet thick, so that we had an immediate result to look at, to contemplate with awe. Some of the evenings T. J. alone was carrying earth up to the building, the rest of the gang distracted by other enterprises or interests, but T. J. kept plugging along on his own and eventually we'd all come back to him again and then our own little acre would grow more rapidly.

He was careful about the kind of dirt he'd let us carry up there and more than once he dumped a sandy load over the parapet into the areaway below because it wasn't good enough. He found out the kinds of earth in all the vacant lots for blocks around. He'd pick it up and feel it and smell it, frozen though it was sometimes, and then he'd say it was good growing soil or it wasn't worth anything and we'd have to go on somewhere else.

Thinking about it now I don't see how he kept us at it. It was hard work, lugging paper sacks and boxes of dirt all the way up the stairs of our own building, keeping out of the way of grownups so they wouldn't catch on to what we were doing. They probably wouldn't have cared, for they didn't pay much attention to us, but we wanted to keep it secret anyway. Then we had to go through the trap door to our roof, teeter over a plank to the fire escape, then climb two or three stories to the parapet and drop down onto the roof. All that for a small pile of earth that sometimes didn't seem worth the effort. But T. J. kept the vision bright within us, his words shrewd and calculated toward the fulfillment of his dream; and he worked harder than any of us. He seemed driven toward a goal that we couldn't see, a particular point in time that would be definitely marked by signs and wonders that only he could see.

The laborious earth just lay there during the cold months, inert and lifeless, the clods lumpy and cold under our feet when we walked over it. But one day it rained and afterward there was a softness in the air and the earth was live and giving again with moisture and warmth. That evening T. J. smelled the air, his nostrils dilating with the odor of the earth under his feet.

"It's spring," he said, and there was a gladness rising in his voice that filled us all with the same feeling. "It's mighty late for it, but it's spring. I'd just about decided it wasn't never gonna get here at all."

We were all sniffing at the air, too, trying to smell it the way T. J. did, and I can still remember the sweet odor of the earth under our feet. It was the first time in my life that spring and spring earth had meant anything to me. I looked at T. J. then, knowing in a faint way the hunger within him through the toilsome winter months, knowing the dream that lay behind his plan. He was a new Antaeus, preparing his own bed of strength.

"Planting time," he said. "We'll have to find us some seed."

"What do we do?" Blackie said. "How do we do it?"

"First we'll have to break up the clods," T. J. said. "That won't be hard to do. Then we plant the seed and after a while they come up. Then you got a crop." He frowned. "But you ain't raised it yet. You got to tend it and hoe it and take care of it, and all the time it's growing and growing while you're awake and while you're asleep. Then you lay it by when it's growed and let it ripen and then you got you a crop."

"There's those wholesale seed houses over on Sixth," I said. "We could probably swipe some grass seed over there."

T. J. looked at the earth. "You-all seem mighty

set on raising some grass," he said. "I ain't never put no effort into that. I spent all my life trying not to raise grass."

"But it's pretty," Blackie said. "We could play on it and take sunbaths on it. Like having our own lawn. Lots of people got lawns."

"Well," T. J. said. He looked at the rest of us, hesitant for the first time. He kept on looking at us for a moment. "I did have it in mind to raise some corn and vegetables. But we'll plant grass."

He was smart. He knew where to give in. And I don't suppose it made any difference to him really. He just wanted to grow something, even if it was grass.

"Of course," he said, "I do think we ought to plant a row of watermelons. They'd be mighty nice to eat while we was a-lying on that grass."

We all laughed. "All right," I said. "We'll plant us a row of watermelons."

Things went very quickly then. Perhaps half the roof was covered with the earth, the half that wasn't broken by ventilators, and we swiped pocketsful of grass seed from the open bins in the wholesale seed house, mingling among the buyers on Saturdays and during the school lunch hour. T. J. showed us how to prepare the earth, breaking up the clods and smoothing it and sowing the grass seed. It looked rich and black now with moisture, receiving of the seed, and it seemed that the grass sprang up overnight, pale green in the early spring.

We couldn't keep from looking at it, unable to believe that we had created this delicate growth. We looked at T. J. with understanding now, knowing the fulfillment of the plan he carried alone within his mind. We had worked without full understanding of the task but he had known all the time.

We found that we couldn't walk or play on the delicate blades, as we had expected to, but we didn't mind. It was enough just to look at it, to realize that it was the work of our own hands, and each evening the whole gang was there, trying to measure the growth that had been achieved that day.

One time a foot was placed on the plot of ground . . . one time only Blackie stepping onto it with sudden bravado. Then he looked at the crushed blades and there was shame in his face. He did not do it again. This was his grass, too, and not to be desecrated. No one said anything, for it was not necessary.

T. J. had reserved a small section for watermelons and he was still trying to find some seed for it. The wholesale house didn't have any watermelon seed and we didn't know where we could lay our hands on any. T. J. shaped the earth into mounds, ready to receive them, three mounds lying in a straight line along the edge of the grass plot.

We had just about decided that we'd have to buy the seed if we were to get them. It was a violation of our principles but we were anxious to get the watermelons started. Somewhere or other, T. J. got his hands on a seed catalogue and brought it one evening to our roof garden.

"We can order them now," he said, showing us the catalogue. "Look!"

We all crowded around, looking at the fat, green watermelons pictured in full color on the pages. Some of them were split open, showing the red, tempting meat, making our mouths water.

"Now we got to scrape up some seed money," T. J. said, looking at us. "I got a quarter. How much you-all got?"

We made up a couple of dollars between us and T. J. nodded his head. "That'll be more than enough. Now we got to decide what kind to get. I think them Kleckley Sweets. What do you-all think?"

He was going into esoteric matters beyond our reach. We hadn't even known there were different kinds of melons. So we just nodded our heads and agreed that yes, we thought the Kleckley Sweets too.

"I'll order them tonight," T. J. said. "We ought to have them in a few days."

Then an adult voice said behind us: "What are you boys doing up here?"

It startled us for no one had ever come up here before, in all the time we had been using the roof of the factory. We jerked around and saw three men standing near the trap door at the other end of the roof. They weren't policemen, or night watchmen, but three plump men in business suits, looking at us. They walked toward us.

"What are you boys doing up here?" the one in the middle said again.

We stood still, guilt heavy among us, levied by the tone of voice, and looked at the three strangers.

The men stared at the grass flourishing behind us. "What's this?" the man said. "How did this get up here?"

"Sure is growing good, ain't it?" T. J. said conversationally. "We planted it."

The men kept looking at the grass as if they didn't believe it. It was a thick carpet over the earth now, a patch of deep greenness startling in the sterile industrial surroundings.

"Yes, sir," T. J. said proudly. "We toted that earth up here and planted that grass." He fluttered the seed catalogue. "And we're just fixing to plant us some watermelon."

The man looked at him then, his eyes strange and faraway. "What do you mean, putting this on the roof of my building?" he said. "Do you want to go to jail?"

T. J. looked shaken. The rest of us were silent, frightened by the authority of his voice. We had grown up aware of adult authority, of policemen and night watchmen and teachers, and this man sounded like all the others. But it was a new thing to T. J.

"Well, you wan't using the roof," T. J. said. He paused a moment and added shrewdly, "so we thought to pretty it up a little bit."

"And sag it so I'd have to rebuild it," the man said sharply. He turned away, saying to a man beside him. "See that all that junk is shoveled off by tomorrow."

"Yes, sir," the man said.

T. J. started forward. "You can't do that," he said. "We toted it up here and it's our earth. We planted it and raised it and toted it up here."

The man stared at him coldly. "But it's my building," he said. "It's to be shoveled off tomorrow."

"It's our earth," T. J. said desperately. "You ain't got no right!"

The man walked on without listening and descended clumsily through the trap door. T. J. stood looking after them, his body tense with anger, until they had disappeared. They wouldn't even argue with him, wouldn't let him defend his earth-rights.

He turned to us. "We won't let 'em do it," he said fiercely. "We'll stay up here all day tomorrow and the day after that and we won't let 'em do it."

We just looked at him. We knew that there was no stopping it. He saw it in our faces and his face wavered for a moment before he gripped it into determination.

"They ain't got no right," he said. "It's our earth. It's our land. Can't nobody touch a man's own land."

We kept on looking at him, listening to the words but knowing that it was no use. The adult world had descended on us even in our richest dream and we knew there was no calculating the adult world, no fighting it, no winning against it.

We started moving slowly toward the parapet and the fire escape, avoiding a last look at the green beauty of the earth that T. J. had planted for us . . . had planted deeply in our minds as well as in our experience. We filed slowly over the edge and down the steps to the plank, T. J.

coming last, and all of us could feel the weight of his grief behind us.

"Wait a minute," he said suddenly, his voice harsh with the effort of calling. We stopped and turned, held by the tone of his voice, and looked up at him standing above us on the fire escape.

"We can't stop them?" he said, looking down at us, his face strange in the dusky light. "There ain't no way to stop 'em?"

"No," Blackie said with finality. "They own the building."

He stood still for a moment, looking up at T. J. caught into inaction by the decision working in his face. He stared back at us and his face was pale and mean in the poor light, with a bald nakedness in his skin like cripples have sometimes.

"They ain't gonna touch my earth," he said fiercely. "They ain't gonna lay a hand on it! Come on."

He turned around and started up the fire escape again, almost running against the effort of climbing. We followed more slowly, not knowing what he intended. By the time we reached him, he had seized a board and thrust it into the soil, scooping it up and flinging it over the parapet into the areaway below. He straightened and looked us squarely in the face.

"They can't touch it," he said. "I won't let 'em lay a dirty hand on it!"

We saw it then. He stooped to his labor again and we followed, the gusts of his anger moving in frenzied labor among us as we scattered along the edge of earth, scooping it and throwing it over the parapet, destroying with anger the growth we had nurtured with such tender care. The soil carried so laboriously upward to the light and the sun cascaded swiftly into the dark areaway, the green glades of grass crumpled and twisted in the falling.

It took less time than you would think . . . the task of destruction is infinitely easier than that of creation. We stopped at the end, leaving only a scattering of loose soil, and when it was finally over a stillness stood among the group and over the factory building. We looked down at the bare sterility of black tar, felt the harsh texture of it under the soles of our shoes, and the anger had gone out of us, leaving only a sore aching in our minds like overstretched muscles.

T. J. stooped for a moment, his breathing slowing from anger and effort, caught into the same contemplation of destruction as all of us. He stooped slowly, finally, and picked up a lonely blade of grass left trampled under our feet and put it between his teeth tasting it, sucking the greenness out of it into his mouth. Then he started walking toward the fire escape, moving before any of us were ready to move, and disappeared over the edge while we stared after him.

We followed him but he was already halfway down to the ground, going on past the board where we crossed over, climbing down into the areaway. We saw the last section swing down with his weight and then he stood on the concrete below us, looking at the small pile of anonymous earth scattered by our throwing. Then he walked across the place where we could see him and disappeared toward the street without glancing back, without looking up to see us watching him.

They did not find him for two weeks. Then the Nashville police caught him just outside the Nashville freight yards. He was walking along the railroad track; still heading south, still heading home.

As for us, who had no remembered home to call us . . . none of us ever again climbed the escape-way to the roof.

EXCHANGE OF MEN
HOWARD NEMEROV and
W. R. JOHNSON

WHEN THE TRAIN PULLED SLOWLY out of Grand
Central, Francis Baron took the miniature chessboard from his pocket and began to contemplate
it. He did not set out the pieces, but simply
studied the sixty-four black and red squares on
which, you might say, he played not only chess
but his whole life as well. Already as he watched
the vacant board, invisible pieces moved and
combined in his mind's eye, developing of themselves the studied complexities of his games. It
was as he had once said, "When one passes a
certain stage, one no longer moves the pieces,
but simply watches them move." Francis Baron

had passed that stage by the time he was twenty years old. What he was doing now, and expected to be doing until the train reached Boston, might be compared to the five-finger exercises which a virtuoso performs faithfully every day. A discipline, a regimen, and more: he knew that from these simple diversions might come the inspiration that would save a game, the subtle but definite variation that had never appeared in books. It had happened so before, and the books had modified themselves agreeably: "The following brilliant line of play was employed for the first time in any tournament by the American master, Francis Baron. . . ."

Now, at the age of forty, on his way to the International Tournament, his appearance certainly suggested nothing so artistic and out of the way as a chess master. He was a small man, neatly but not distinctively dressed, and his only peculiarity was a rather oversized round head from which large eyes peered through silver-rimmed glasses. This anonymity of appearance, coupled with his magnificent play, had caused someone to nickname him "the mighty pawn," a title which, with that other more grandiose one of "master," he had retained since his early tournaments.

Conductors and people passing through the car glanced curiously at the little man who nursed in his lap the unoccupied chessboard as though it were a treasure or a secret sorrow; and a personable young man, who sat with a pretty girl across the aisle, leaned over and asked, "Would you care to have a game?"

Baron looked up in some annoyance. "Thank you, no," he said primly, and, while he spoke, he exchanged queens with his invisible opponent, and came out with the advantage of a pawn. That was one thing about being a master: you could not play with anybody you happened to meet. Even a master dropped games surprisingly often, and such a loss to an unknown opponent in a railroad car would be embarrassing, not to mention the detriment to one's reputation. Also, though Baron was a young man compared to most of the masters he would meet in tournament play, he already had a strong respect, which soon would become fear, for the rising generation. He himself must have looked like a naive innocent when, at twenty-three, he defeated Orimund in the first of many games. Now he could not blame Orimund for behaving so ungraciously afterward.

Fearing he might have been rude, he said now, "I'm terribly busy, you see," and realized that it must have sounded ridiculous.

"Are you going to watch the tournament in Boston?" the young man asked.

Baron hesitated. "Yes," he said finally. "Yes, I expect to be there." Firmly his mind told him, rook takes rook, pawn takes rook, check . . . the ending would be simplicity itself.

"I guess it's really between Orimund, Savard, and Baron," said the young man. "No one else has much chance against those three."

The mate, Baron thought, would be accomplished with a very small force, because the white king was blocked in three directions by his own pawns.

"I admire Orimund very much," the young man continued. "He's the last of the old grand masters. He has the most intense attack I've ever seen. I rather hope he becomes champion again. It would be a victory not only for himself, but for his style of play as well."

"You don't much care for the modern way?" asked Baron.

"Too much subtlety, too much caution," said the young man. "Modern chess isn't playing; it's waiting."

"It wins."

"Look," the young man offered. "How about a game? I'll spot you whatever you like—a rook, even."

Baron smiled. "I don't think that will be necessary."

"Well, I feel I should tell you; I'm Richard James, that is—I don't suppose you've heard of me although I was the winner of the intercollegiate championship last year."

So this was Richard James. Baron remembered a piece in the papers, not about the intercollegiate tournament, but about another, a small affair in Chicago, in which a young man named Richard James had lost rather badly to Max Tarnes, but had carried off the brilliancy prize all the same for a rather exciting combination against

Jacob Goldman. He could see the familiar old pattern as it began to repeat itself. In a year, or two years, or three, he would be facing the brilliant young master, Richard James, across the tournament board, and everything would be at stake. But nothing need be given away at this moment. He began to set up the pieces.

"I'd still prefer to play even," he said.

"Now are you satisfied?" asked the pretty girl. "You've trapped the innocent bystander into a game. That's what's such fun about being married to Dick," she explained to Baron, "You meet such a lot of interesting people. But by a strange coincidence, they all play chess."

The young man laughed. "I want you to meet my wife, Sally, Mr. — ?"

Baron looked at the board. "Springer, John Springer," he said, using the German name for knight. His use of a pseudonym, he told himself, was not in the least disreputable. After all, he had a standing which must be jealously guarded. Suppose there should be a slip, an accident, the distraction of being aboard a rattling train, the disturbingly informal conditions generally — he did not intend that such an accident should affect the reputation or the tournament play of Francis Baron during the next week.

But in trying temporarily, at least, to conceal his identity, he must not, he knew, employ his own style of play, which to an expert would at once reveal both his name and his quality. He must accept, then the disadvantage of meeting

Richard James on the latter's own ground, which would probably be the ground of a violent attack, initiated as rapidly as possible. Ordinarily, Baron would withdraw before such an attack and use his whole development for defense, for subtle probing and slow exploiting of weaknesses, occupying more and more space in the long wait for his opponent's critical mistake, which must come in time. Then, rapidly, the complexion of the match would change. From the reticence of his beginnings and his control of strategic area, Baron would open out the penetrating, incisive, and fatal counterattack. That was the way, the modern style, which had made Baron a master. But now he must fight by older and riskier methods.

Young James drew the white and opened with the Max Lange attack, quick and straight down the center of the board. It was evident he was trying for immediate victory, and accepting a disadvantageous position if the attempt failed.

Baron countered along conventional lines, vigorously fighting for the center, for the points from which well-masked and defended powers could extend their grasp on positions within the enemy's lines. Both men were slightly nervous. There was a quality of chess, thought Baron, which made it absurd to say, "It's only a game." On the contrary, as you could judge from the way people played it, it was a warlike and representative struggle for mastery. It was a conspectus of life itself, with the illusion of power over life, which is why, though unthinking people laugh to hear of it, the chess master often dies worn out, overstrained from an incredible depth and complexity of concentration prolonged over a period of years.

As they entered the end game with an exchange of queens, James was a pawn behind, but occupied better immediate attacking position.

"You play extremely well, sir," he said deferentially to Baron, who nodded and smiled. The position, he saw, was critical. If Richard James possessed perfect book knowledge, he had what amounted to a winning game. On the other hand, he was nervous, just about trembling with eagerness for success. If that nervousness could be exploited properly, or improperly, for that matter, but exploited somehow — Francis Baron regretted exceedingly having been drawn into the match. This young man would be present at the tournament; he would recognize his opponent of the railroad car; there would surely be some publicity. He could imagine Savard's wry, crooked grin; and not alone Savard. Baron was not so well liked among the masters; they resented his youth and perhaps his manner as well. There would be a good deal of laughter over this.

Abruptly he said, "I'm afraid I didn't tell you my real name." He smiled in apology, held out his hand. "I'm Francis Baron."

On the surface it was all right. It was even a

compliment to the younger man. The master, by revealing his identity, seemed to be acknowledging a worthy opponent. And Richard James tried desperately to take the acknowledgment in that spirit. But there was now too much at stake. He was no longer playing a chess game. He was playing, with a chance to win, against Francis Baron himself. He blushed and stammered, "I hope you didn't think me rude — about Orimund, I mean. I had no idea — "

"Of course not." Francis Baron smiled. "Orimund plays his way, I play mine. It's your move, Mr. James."

Two moves later, Richard James moved the pawn that cost him the game. His famous antagonist was gracious in triumph, quiet and assured as he complimented the younger man on playing a very strong game.

"We shall be seeing you in tournament play very soon, I fear," he said cordially when they parted in Back Bay Station.

"You're very kind to say so; we look forward to watching your games."

Both men knew what had happened. For Baron the victory was rather empty, achieved by a trick in a class with blowing smoke in your opponent's face throughout a game (this being the favorite stratagem of one Russian master), or whistling, or tapping your fingers on the table. And worst of all, he did not know if he could have won that particular game without such a device.

As for Richard James, he said to his wife, "I don't know why he had to pick that moment to tell me who he was. I was doing all right until then, but Lord — to be up against Francis Baron! I just collapsed right there."

"And that," said Sally, "is just about what he wanted. Your Francis Baron may be a great master, but it strikes me he's just a little bit of a heel at the same time."

"Now, darling, he could have beaten me anyhow."

"Don't 'now darling' me. I don't know much about chess, and he may have been able to beat you hollow; but from what I saw of his face at the time, he didn't think so."

The players in the tournament, thought Baron, had all the solemnity and high seriousness of a conclave of cardinals met to elect a new Pope, and all the jealousy, to be sure, of a boys' ball team electing a captain. It was the first International Tournament since before the war, and the meeting was marked by the absence of a few faces formerly well known: Estignan, who was dead; Zinuccio, who had turned Fascist and was in prison; Enrich, who was not allowed to leave his country. But the others he knew well enough: the English master, Cranley, looking in his rich tweeds like an aged schoolboy; Savard, the Frenchman, a dumpy little man who resembled a chef and played the most eccentric games of any master; Jasoff, from Russia, looking more than usually peaked and unhappy; and several other masters from all over the world. Second-rate, thought Baron. And yet, not really second-rate; so little distance, in chess, separated the master from the expert, the merely brilliant player. It was more than probable, he reflected with distaste, that he would lose games to more than one of them. But fortunately, in a chess tournament one was not eliminated for losing a game. Elimination occurred at definite stages, on the basis of point score: one for a win, one half for a draw. After a complete round, those with the lowest scores went out and the remainder began again.

And there was Orimund, at last. The aged master whose white hair stood out like a wiry halo over his head, who always wore a high white collar and shiny black suit. Orimund, nearing seventy, with his trembling hands, his gentle voice and perfect manners, and that mind whose keenness had probably suffered somewhat during the last years. They said he had spent time in a concentration camp, and looking at him now, Baron found it easy to believe this. He had not remembered the old man so gentle, so meek. They met in the lobby of the hotel, and Orimund seemed to have forgotten his resentment of Baron. They called each other, conventionally, Master, and were for a moment, almost friendly.

"Ach, life passes, Master Baron," the old man said. "You, too, are no longer exactly of the youngsters."

Was that the way of it? Did one creep gently

out of life, shedding the old antagonisms, ridding oneself gradually of the vicious desire for success?

"I am glad to have the honor once again, Master," he replied.

"Perhaps for the last time," Orimund said. "You know, years ago, when I was asked, 'How can you waste your life playing chess?' I was able to reply 'How can you waste your life writing books, or making money, or painting pictures, or whatever?' And it was a good, an acceptable answer. Now, I confess, I begin to wonder, what have I done? I was given my life and what have I made of it?"

"You leave an immortal name," replied Baron gravely.

"An immortal name — better to have died ten years ago, much better. Perhaps you will understand that someday, Master." This last, Baron recognized, was said with the familiar, cold, deadly anger that he remembered as an element in the former Orimund. But Baron understood what the old man meant: better to have died champion of the world, rather than face the failing of one's powers, the uprising of the young just when one is no longer able to oppose them with success. Better than the last cold years in which, if a master makes a mistake, he believes himself to be losing his mind.

That was the last time they spoke together except over the board. Almost angrily, Baron put down the pity he felt for the old genius. If that's the way it is, that's all, he told himself. When my time comes, I don't expect to weep on the conqueror's shoulder. That's what life is, and if we were the same age I would still be confident of winning. For that matter, if the position were reversed, would he show any mercy to me? I doubt it.

The tournament was not easy. Few can go through the nervous strain of game after game against excellent players without feeling a sense of desperation, and Francis Baron was no exception. The competition grew progressively more severe, and in the last matches of the opening round one came up against players who, knowing already that they would be eliminated, played with violence and extravagance in the hope of taking home by way of consolation at least one victory over a possible world's champion. Baron was beaten in this way by Jasoff and Cranley, while Orimund dropped games to Savard and Baron himself.

Baron, however, was superbly confident. In the first round he had beaten Savard, and his victory over Orimund was achieved, if not easily, at least with certainty and power from the opening move of a solid, invulnerable game. The old man played with a brilliance matching his former great tournament play, but finding his attack met at all points, he overextended his defenses slightly and was unable to withstand the vicious counterattack when it finally came.

Richard and Sally were present at all his

matches, and though Baron did not in any way acknowledge their interest, he felt intensely and uncomfortably that they had in some sense seen through what had occurred on the train, that it would give them pleasure if he lost, that they were in fact simply waiting for him to make a mistake. He smiled ironically to himself. There would be no mistakes, there must be none — perfection. And forthwith he proceeded roundly to trounce Dr. Anderson, his last opponent in the first round.

Orimund, Savard, Francis Baron, and an Irishman named Brian alone escaped elimination. In the second round Brian realized suddenly that he was very close to being world's champion, and simply collapsed, losing to everyone. Savard lost to Baron and Orimund, and these last drew their games and entered the final with a score of two and a half each for the round.

On the night before the last match, Baron was sitting in the hotel lobby, reading, when he was approached by the secretary of the local chess club.

"We have about ten people collected," this functionary said, "and we wondered if you'd care to give some sort of exhibition. We would be honored, greatly honored, Master, and I can say definitely that there will be no publicity. Of course, I realize that you may not feel inclined to make the effort on the eve of the final, but I was instructed to ask you all the same." He hesitated, looked apologetic, and seemed, as though realizing the enormity of his request, to be ready to retire without an answer; but Baron stopped him.

"Under the conditions you specify," he said, "I shouldn't object to the exercise. In fact, I'm grateful for the compliment of your interest. But understand, I'll hold you to strict silence on the subject. In the first place, it would be a reflection on my opponent if it got out that I was so careless of him as to play for fun on the night before our game. I can play tonight only if it is understood that the results don't matter, that it is simply a relaxation from the tournament."

"I quite understand," the secretary said. "This is the arrangement. The members will be told that a master, whose name will not be given, will play blindfolded against all ten of them simultaneously. The master will be in a room apart, and will not meet the other players either before or after the match. In that way the secret of your identity can be kept between the president and myself until after tomorrow night. And besides, the other players will be asked to keep silent about the whole event."

These terms proving to Baron's satisfaction, he was driven to the quarters of the Copley Chess Club, where he was placed in a small antechamber and left alone. Presently the secretary came in.

"It has been arranged," he said, "that you are to have white in the even-numbered games and black in the odd. Fair enough?"

"Fair enough," replied Francis Baron.

"Then the first move in all the odd-numbered games is pawn to king four," said the secretary.

"My reply is the same, and my opening move in the even-numbered games is pawn to queen four."

That was the way of it, he thought. In this blindfolded game one allowed the opponents to open up a little, and then when the weak sisters among them disclosed themselves, they must be whipped rapidly, allowing one to concentrate on the difficult games.

The amateurs did show themselves very soon. Games one, two, four, eight, and nine took less than fifteen moves for the establishment of overwhelming superiority on Baron's side. Few of the games were in any way rewarding, except as an exercise in concentration for the master.

At last game number seven sorted itself out from the rest; there was something there. A Max Lange attack, with a curious variation in the placement of the queen's knight. Going over the position in his mind, Baron began to recognize the style. His opponent, he was almost certain, could be no one but Richard James. A few minutes later an astonishingly rapid attack confirmed his belief. Baron felt himself being pressed with some severity and marshaled his forces to defend. It would be a close game.

The other games expired in something over the fortieth move. He had won them all, but then, the competition had been very nearly nothing. The seventh game, however, was close and even threatening. James was playing for a brilliant win and, as things stood, it was well within the possible for him to achieve it. And this time there was no way of breaking the boy's nerve; instead, Baron knew, his own nerve might go. It was so easy to make a mistake; he was holding precariously in his mind the crossing, tangling threads of thirty-two pieces moving altogether more than eighty times over sixty-four squares. The possibilities were infinite. If one forgot a move, or misplaced a move in memory, it was over: defeat. One defeat, of course, in ten blindfold games, is nothing; but to lose to young James! And he was certain that James knew his opponent; he felt an intellectual rapport that enabled him to picture the handsome young face as it bent over the board, and realized that James knew perfectly well that he was playing — and winning — against Francis Baron.

And then it came. The secretary entered, said, "Game number seven. Pawn to bishop six."

"Is he certain of that?" Baron asked.

"That is his move, sir."

"My reply — queen takes rook."

Francis Baron breathed easily. Richard James had made a mistake, a subtle mistake, to be sure, and not immediately apparent, but the master could now foresee the imminent collapse of his opponent's game. After the sacrifice of the queen, the knight and two rooks would accomplish the rest. He called after the secretary, "I announce checkmate in six moves."

It went as he planned, now. On the fifth move he forced the white rook to occupy the square adjacent to the white king, thus blocking all escape squares and enabling the knight to mate at bishop seven. He returned to his hotel.

But he was troubled in his mind. A mistake like that, it was unnatural, considering how masterful James' play had been up until then. It was tantamount to deliberate surrender, it was . . . it was deliberate surrender! He saw it now. James had recognized his adversary, had realized that Baron, strained by the tournament, could be upset beyond measure by a defeat of any sort at this moment, and he had deliberately opened up his board so as to be defeated. It was a gesture of the most subtle and keen sportsmanship; it was, in a way, a moral revelation. After all, he reflected, when you consider that he probably dislikes me intensely, and realized that he had it in his power to hurt my game and refrained — that shows the greatest delicacy.

Francis Baron found it difficult to get to sleep. His own face kept appearing to him saying, "I am Francis Baron, I am Francis Baron," over and over with the utmost pomposity imaginable. What was it for? he asked himself. For a game of chess. Chess is not, after all, life itself. Chess, if you regard it properly, is a game. A great game, true; but is it worth the demands it makes? Fancy a man like Orimund, now decrepit, feeling bitterly the decline of his powers, yet playing with the most religious courage.

He could imagine Orimund after the final match, returning alone to Europe. There would still be many admirers, would still be the satisfaction of a good game, not a great game, mind; but deeply, essentially, he would be an old man, nearing death, alone.

Orimund won the final game. Francis Baron would never forget how the reporters gathered around after the game, nor how the old man wept far more over his success than he would have wept over his defeat. And how Orimund called him "Master" and said good-bye in the most touching and friendly way, his hand on the younger man's shoulder. "After me," he had said, "in a year, less perhaps, who knows?"

Between dejection and satisfaction, Francis Baron, runner-up for the world's chess championship, packed his bag and prepared to return to New York. The analysis of that final game, he knew, would give many people reason enough to laugh at him.

"Come in," he said in response to a knock.

Richard and Sally James stood at the door. He invited them in, and Richard said, "We just wanted you to know we saw what you did in that game." Sally nodded in agreement. "And we'd like to tell you we thought it was wonderful."

"Did? I didn't do anything — except lose, of course."

"You gave him the game. You did it purposely, and you did it so that no one who didn't know both your styles perfectly would ever realize."

Francis Baron smiled at them. "There's no need to shout it all over the place," he said. "Anyhow, I've got you to thank for my quixotic behavior. You taught me a great deal about games and other things last night."

"Last night?" James looked blank.

"Yes. At the Copley Club, you know. Game number seven."

"I don't get it," Richard James said. "I've never been to the Copley Club in my life."

FLOWERS FOR ALGERNON

DANIEL KEYES

progris riport 1—martch 5, 1965

Dr Strauss says I shud rite down what I think and evrey thing that happins to me from now on. I dont know why but he says its importint so they will see if they will use me. I hope they use me. Miss Kinnian says maybe they can make me smart. I want to be smart. My name is Charley Gordon. I am 37 years old. I have nuthing more to rite now so I will close for today.

progris riport 2—martch 6

I had a test today. I think I faled it. And I think maybe now they wont use me. What happind is a nice young man was in the room and he had some white cards and ink spilled all over them. He sed Charlie what do you see on this

card. I was very skared even tho I had my
rabits foot in my pockit because when I was a
kid I always faled tests in school and I spilled
ink to.

I told him I saw a inkblot. He said yes and
and it made me feel good. I thot that was all
but when I got up to go he said Charlie we
are not thru yet. Then I dont remember so good
but he wantid me to say what was in the ink.
I dint see nuthing in the ink but he said there
was picturs there other pepul saw some picturs.
I couldnt see any picturs. I reely tryed. I held
the card close up and then far away. Then I
said if I had my glasses I could see better I
usally only ware my glasses in the movies or TV
but I said they are in the closit in the hall. I
got them. Then I said let me see that card agen
I bet Ill find it now.

I tryed hard but I only saw the ink. I told
him maybe I need new glasses. He rote something down on a paper and I got skared of fal-
ing the test. I told him it was a very nice inkblot with littel points all around the edges. He
looked very sad so that wasnt it. I said please
let me try agen. Ill get it in a few minits becaus
Im not so fast sometimes. Im a slow reeder too
in Miss Kinnians class for slow adults but Im
trying very hard.

He gave me a chance with another card that
had 2 kinds of ink spilled on it red and blue.

He was very nice and talked slow like Miss
Kinnian does and he explaned it to me that it
was a *raw shok*. He said pepul see things in the
ink. I said show me where. He said think. I

told him I think a inkblot but that wasnt rite eather. He said what does it remind you—pretend something. I closed my eyes for a long time to pretend. I told him I pretend a fowntan pen with ink leeking all over a table cloth.

I don't think I passed the *raw shok* test.

progris riport 3—martch 7

Dr Strauss and Dr Nemur say it dont matter about the inkblots. They said that maybe they will still use me. I said Miss Kinnian never gave me tests like that one only spelling and reading. They said Miss Kinnian told that I was her bestist pupil in the adult nite school becaus I tryed the hardist and I reely wantid to lern. They said how come you went to the adult nite scool all by yourself Charlie. How did you find it. I said I asked pepul and sumbody told me where I shud go to lern to read and spell good. They said why did you want to. I told them becaus all my life I wantid to be smart and not dumb. But its very hard to be smart. They said you know it will probably be tempirery. I said yes. Miss Kinnian told me. I dont care if it herts.

Later I had more crazy tests today. The nice lady who gave it to me told me the name and I asked her how do you spellit so I can rite it in my progris riport. THEMATIC APPERCEPTION TEST. I dont know the frist 2 words but I know what *test* means. You got to pass it or you get bad marks. This test lookd easy becaus I coud see the picturs. Only this time she dint want me to tell her the picturs. That mixd me up. She said make up storys about the pepul in the picturs.

I told her how can you tell storys about pepul you never met. I said why shud I make up lies. I never tell lies any more becaus I always get caut.

She told me this test and the other one the raw shok was for getting personality. I laffed so hard. I said how can you get that thing from inkblots and fotos. She got sore and put her picturs away. I don't care. It was sily. I gess I faled that test too.

Later some men in white coats took me to a difernt part of the hospitil and gave me a game to play. It was like a race with a white mouse. They called the mouse Algernon. Algernon was in a box with a lot of twists and turns like all kinds of walls and they gave me a pencil and a paper with lines and lots of boxes. On one side it said START and on the other end it said FINISH. They said it was *amazed* and that Algernon and me had the same *amazed* to do. I dint see how we could have the same *amazed* if Algernon had a box and I had a paper but I dint say nothing. Anyway there wasnt time because the race started.

One of the men had a watch he was trying to hide so I wouldnt see it so I tryed not to look and that made me nervus.

Anyway that test made me feel worser than all the others because they did it over 10 times with different *amazeds* and Algernon won every time. I dint know that mice were so smart. Maybe thats because Algernon is a white mouse. Maybe white mice are smarter than other mice.

progris riport 4—Mar 8

Their going to use me! Im so exited I can hardly write. Dr Nemur and Dr Strauss had a argament about it first. Dr Nemur was in the office when Dr Strauss brot me in. Dr Nemur was worryed about using me but Dr Strauss told him Miss Kinnian rekemmended me the best from all the people who she was teaching. I like Miss Kinnian becaus shes a very smart teacher. And she said Charlie your going to have a second chance. If you volenteer for this experament you mite get smart. They dont know if it will be perminint but theirs a chance. Thats why I said ok even when I was scared because she said it was an operashun. She said dont be scared Charlie you done so much with so little I think you deserv it most of all.

So I got scaird when Dr Nemur and Dr Strauss argud about it. Dr Strauss said I had something that was very good. He said I had a good *motorvation*. I never even knew I had that. I felt proud when he said that not every body with an eye-q of 68 had that thing. I dont know what it is or where I got it but he said Algernon had it too. Algernons *motorvation* is the cheese they put in his box. But it cant be that because I didnt eat any cheese this week.

Then he told Dr Nemur something I dint understand so while they were talking I wrote down some of the words.

He said Dr Nemur I know Charlie is not what you had in mind as the first of your new brede of intelek** (coudnt get the word) superman. But most people of his low ment** are host** and uncoop** they are usually dull apath** and hard to reach. He has a good natcher hes intristed and eager to please.

Dr Nemur said remember he will be the first human beeng ever to have his intelijence tripled by surgicle meens.

Dr Strauss said exakly. Look at how well hes lerned to read and write for his low mentel age its as grate an acheve** as you and I lerning einstines therey of **vity without help. That shows the inteness motorvation. Its comparat** a tremen** achev** I say we use Charlie.

I dint get all the words but it sounded like Dr Strauss was on my side and like the other one wasnt.

Then Dr Nemur nodded he said allright maybe your right. We will use Charlie. When he said that I got so exited I jumped up and shook his hand for being so good to me. I told him thank you doc you wont be sorry for giving me a second chance. And I mean it like I told him. After the operashun Im gonna try to be smart. Im gonna try awful hard.

progris riport 5—Mar 10

Im skared. Lots of the nurses and the people who gave me the tests came to bring me candy and wish me luck. I hope I have luck. I got my rabits foot and my lucky penny. Only a black cat crossed me when I was comming to the hospitil. Dr Strauss says dont be supersitis Charlie this is science. Anyway Im keeping my rabits foot with me.

I asked Dr Strauss if Ill beat Algernon in the race after the operashun and he said maybe. If the operashun works Ill show that mouse I can be as smart as he is. Maybe smarter. Then Ill be abel to read better and spell the words good and know lots of things and be like other people. I want to be smart like other people. If it works perminint they will make everybody smart all over the wurld.

They dint give me anything to eat this morning. I dont know what that eating has to do with getting smart. Im very hungry and Dr Nemur took away my box of candy. That Dr Nemur is a grouch. Dr Strauss says I can have it back after the operashun. You cant eat befor a operashun . . .

progress report 6—Mar 15

The operashun dint hurt. He did it while I was sleeping. They took off the bandijis from my head today so I can make a PROGRESS REPORT. Dr Nemur who looked at some of my other ones says I spell PROGRESS wrong and told me how to spell it and REPORT too. I got to try and remember that.

I have a very bad memary for spelling. Dr Strauss says its ok to tell about all the things that happin to me but he says I should tell more about what I feel and what I think. When I told him I dont know how to think he said try. All the time when the bandijis were on my eyes I tryed to think. Nothing happened. I dont know what to think about. Maybe if I ask him he will tell me how I can think now that Im suppose to get smart. What do smart people think about. Fancy things I suppose. I wish I knew some fancy things alredy.

progress report 7—mar 19

Nothing is happining. I had lots of tests and different kinds of races with Algernon. I hate that mouse. He always beats me. Dr Strauss said I got to play those games. And he said some time I got to take those tests over again. Those inkblots are stupid. And those pictures are stupid too. I like to draw a picture of a man and a woman but I wont make up lies about people.

I got a headache from trying to think so much. I thot Dr Strauss was my friend but he dont help me. He dont tell me what to think or when Ill get smart. Miss Kinnian dint come to see me. I think writing these progress reports are stupid too.

progress report 8—Mar 23

Im going back to work at the factery. They said it was better I shud go back to work but I cant tell anyone what the operashun was for and I have to come to the hospitil for an hour evry night after work. They are gonna pay me mony every month for learning to be smart.

Im glad Im going back to work because I

miss my job and all my friends and all the fun we have there.

Dr Strauss says I shud keep writing things down but I dont have to do it every day just when I think of something or something speshul happins. He says dont get discoridged because it takes time and it happins slow. He says it took a long time with Algernon before he got 3 times smarter than he was before. Thats why Algernon beats me all the time because he had that operashun too. That makes me feel better. I could probly do that *amazed* faster than a reglar mouse. Maybe some day Ill beat him. That would be something. So far Algernon looks smart perminent.

Mar 25 (I don't have to write PROGRESS REPORT on top any more just when I hand it in once a week for Dr Nemur. I just have to put the date on. That saves time)

We had a lot of fun at the factory today. Joe Carp said hey look where Charlie had his operashun what did they do Charlie put some brains in. I was going to tell him but I remembered Dr Strauss said no. Then Frank Reilly said what did you do Charlie forget your key and open your door the hard way. That made me laff. Their really my friends and they like me.

Sometimes somebody will say hey look at Joe or Frank or George he really pulled a Charlie Gordon. I dont know why they say that but they always laff. This morning Amos Borg who is the 4 man at Donnegans used my name when he shouted at Ernie the office boy. Ernie lost a packige. He said Ernie for godsake what are you trying to be a Charlie Gordon. I dont understand why he said that.

Mar 28 Dr Strauss came to my room tonight to see why I dint come in like I was suppose to. I told him I dont like to race with Algernon any more. He said I dont have to for a while but I shud come in. He had a present for me. I thot it was a little television but it wasnt. He said I got to turn it on when I go to sleep. I said your kidding why shud I turn it on when Im going to sleep. Who ever herd of a thing like that. But he said if I want to get smart I got to do what he says. I told him I dint think I was going to get smart and he puts his hand on my sholder and said Charlie you dont know it yet but your getting smarter all the time. You wont notice for a while. I think he was just being nice to make me feel good because I dont look any smarter.

Oh yes I almost forgot. I asked him when I can go back to the class at Miss Kinnians school. He said I wont go their. He said that soon Miss Kinnian will come to the hospital to start and teach me speshul.

Mar 29 That crazy TV kept up all night. How can I sleep with something yelling crazy things all night in my ears. And the nutty pictures. Wow. I don't know what it says when Im up so how am I going to know when Im sleeping.

Dr Strauss says its ok. He says my brains are lerning when I sleep and that will help me when Miss Kinnian starts my lessons in the hospitl (only I found out it isn't a hospitl its a labatory.) I think its all crazy. If you can get smart when your sleeping why do people go to school. That thing I don't think will work. I use to watch the late show and the late late show on TV all the time and it never made me smart. Maybe you have to sleep while you watch it.

progress report 9—April 3

Dr Strauss showed me how to keep the TV turned low so now I can sleep. I dont hear a thing. And I still dont understand what it says. A few times I play it over in the morning to find out what I lerned when I was sleeping and I dont think so. Miss Kinnian says Maybe its another langwidge. But most times it sounds american. It talks faster than even Miss Gold who was my teacher in 6 grade.

I told Dr Strauss what good is it to get smart in my sleep. I want to be smart when Im awake. He says its the same thing and I have two minds. Theres the *subconscious* and the *conscious* (thats how you spell it). And one dont tell the other one what its doing. They don't even talk to each other. Thats why I dream. And boy have I been having crazy dreams. Wow. Ever since that night TV. The late late late show.

I forgot to ask him if it was only me or if everybody had those two minds.

(I just looked up the word in the dictionary Dr Strauss gave me. The word is *subconscious. adj. Of the nature of mental operations yet not present in consciousness; as, subconscious conflict of desires.*) There's more but I still dont know what it means. This isnt a very good dictionary for dumb people like me.

Anyway the headache is from the party. My friends from the factery Joe Carp and Frank Reilly invited me to go to Muggsys Saloon for some drinks. I dont like to drink but they said we will have lots of fun. I had a good time.

Joe Carp said I shoud show the girls how I mop out the toilet in the factory and he got me a mop. I showed them and everyone laffed when I told that Mr. Donnegan said I was the best jeniter he ever had because I like my job and do it good and never miss a day except for my operashun.

I said Miss Kinnian always said Charlie be proud of your job because you do it good.

Everybody laffed and we had a good time and they gave me lots of drinks and Joe said Charlie is a card when hes potted. I dont know what that means but everybody likes me and we have fun. I cant wait to be smart like my best friends Joe Carp and Frank Reilly.

I dont remember how the party was over but I think I went out to buy a newspaper and coffee for Joe and Frank and when I came back there was no one their. I looked for them all over till late. Then I dont remember so good but I think I got sleepy or sick. A nice cop brot me back home. Thats what my landlady Mrs Flynn says.

But I got a headache and a big lump on my head. I think maybe I fell but Joe Carp says it was the cop they beat up drunks some times. I don't think so. Miss Kinnian says cops are to help people. Anyway I got a bad headache and Im sick and hurt all over. I dont think Ill drink anymore.

April 6 I beat Algernon! I dint even know I beat him until Burt the tester told me. Then the second time I lost because I got so exited I fell off the chair before I finished. But after that I beat him 8 more times. I must be getting smart to beat a smart mouse like Algernon. But I dont *feel* smarter.

I wanted to race Algernon some more but Burt said that was enough for one day. They let me hold him for a minit. Hes not so bad. Hes soft like a ball of cotton. He blinks and when he opens his eyes their black and pink on the eges.

I said can I feed him because I felt bad to beat him and I wanted to be nice and make friends. Burt said no Algernon is a very specshul mouse with an operashun like mine, and he was the first of all the animals to stay smart so long. He told me Algernon is so smart that every day he has to solve a test to get his food. Its a thing like a lock on a door that changes every time Algernon goes in to eat so he has to lern something new to get his food. That made me sad because if he coudnt lern he would be hungry.

I don't think its right to make you pass a test to eat. How woud Dr Nemur like it to have to pass a test every time he wants to eat. I think Ill be friends with Algernon.

April 9 Tonight after work Miss Kinnian was at the laboratory. She looked like she was glad to see me but scared. I told her dont worry Miss Kinnian Im not smart yet and she laffed. She said I have confidence in you Charlie the way you struggled so hard to read and right better than all the others. At werst you will have it for a littel wile and your doing something for science.

We are reading a very hard book. Its called *Robinson Crusoe* about a man who gets merooned on a dessert Iland. Hes smart and figers out all kinds of things so he can have a house and food and hes a good swimmer. Only I feel sorry because hes all alone and has no friends. But I think their must be somebody else on the iland because theres a picture with his funny umbrella looking at footprints. I hope he gets a frend and not be lonly.

April 10 Miss Kinnian teaches me to spell better. She says look at a word and close your eyes and say it over and over until you remember. I have lots of trüble with *through* that you say *threw* and *enough* and *tough* that you dont say *enew* and *tew*. You got to say *enuff* and *tuff*. Thats how I use to write it before I started to get smart. Im confused but Miss Kinnian says theres no reason in spelling.

Apr 14 Finished *Robinson Crusoe*. I want to find out more about what happens to him but Miss Kinnian says thats all there is. *Why.*

Apr 15 Miss Kinnian says Im lerning fast. She read some of the Progress Reports and she looked at me kind of funny. She says Im a fine person and Ill show them all. I asked her why. She said never mind but I shouldnt feel bad if I find out everybody isnt nice like I think. She said for a person who god gave so little to you done more than a lot of people with brains they never even used. I said all my friends are smart people but there good. They like me and they never did anything that wasnt nice. Then she got something in her eye and she had to run out to the ladys room.

Apr 16 Today, I lerned, the *comma*, this is a comma (,) a period, with a tail, Miss Kinnian, says its importent, because, it makes writing, better, she said, somebody, coud lose, a lot of money, if a comma, isnt, in the, right place, I don't have, any money, and I dont see, how a comma, keeps you, from losing it,

Apr 17 I used the comma wrong. Its punctuation. Miss Kinnian told me to look up long words in the dictionary to lern to spell them. I said whats the difference if you can read it anyway. She said its part of your education so now on Ill look up all the words Im not sure how to spell. It takes a long time to write that way but I only have to look up once and after that I get it right.

You got to mix them up. She showed? me" how. to mix! them (and now; I can! mix up all kinds" of punctuation, in! my writing? There, are lots! of rules? to lern; but Im gettin'g them in my head.

One thing I like about, Dear Miss Kinnian: (thats the way it goes in a business letter if I ever go into business) is she, always gives me' a reason" when-I ask. She's a gen'ius! I wish I cou'd be smart" like, her;

(Punctuation, is; fun!)

April 18 What a dope I am! I didn't even understand what she was talking about. I read the grammar book last night and it explanes the whole thing. Then I saw it was the same way as Miss Kinnian was trying to tell me, but I didnt get it.

Miss Kinnian said that the TV working in my sleep helped out. She and I reached a plateau. That's a flat hill.

After I figured out how punctuation worked, I read over all my old Progress Reports from the beginning. Boy, did I have crazy spelling and punctuation! I told Miss Kinnian I ought to go over the pages and fix all the mistakes but she said, "No Charlie, Dr. Nemur wants them just as they are. That's why he let you keep them after they were photostated, to see your own progress. You're coming along fast, Charlie."

That made me feel good. After the lesson I went down and played with Algernon. We don't race any more.

April 20 I feel sick inside. Not sick like for a doctor, but inside my chest it feels empty like getting punched and a heartburn at the same time. I wasn't going to write about it, but I guess I got to, because it's important. Today was the first time I ever stayed home from work.

Last night Joe Carp and Frank Reilly invited me to a party. There were lots of girls and some men from the factory. I remembered how sick I got last time I drank too much, so I told Joe I didn't want anything to drink. He gave me a plain Coke instead.

We had a lot of fun for a while. Joe said I

should dance with Ellen and she would teach me the steps. I fell a few times and I couldn't understand why because no one else was dancing besides Ellen and me. And all the time I was tripping because somebody's foot was always sticking out.

Then when I got up I saw the look on Joe's face and it gave me a funny feeling in my stomack. "He's a scream," one of the girls said. Everybody was laughing.

"Look at him. He's blushing. Charlie is blushing."

"Hey, Ellen, what'd you do to Charlie? I never saw him act like that before."

I didn't know what to do or where to turn. Everyone was looking at me and laughing and I felt naked. I wanted to hide. I ran outside and I threw up. Then I walked home. It's a funny thing I never knew that Joe and Frank and the others liked to have me around all the time to make fun of me.

Now I know what it means when they say "to pull a Charlie Gordon."

I'm ashamed.

progress report 11

April 21 Still didn't go into the factory. I told Mrs. Flynn my landlady to call and tell Mr. Donnegan I was sick. Mrs. Flynn looks at me very funny lately like she's scared.

I think it's a good thing about finding out how everybody laughs at me. I thought about it a lot. It's because I'm so dumb and I don't even know when I'm doing something dumb. People think it's funny when person can't do things the same way they can.

Anyway, now I know I'm getting smarter every day. I know punctuation and I can spell good. I like to look up all the hard words in the dictionary and I remember them. I'm reading a lot now, and Miss Kinnian says I read very fast. Sometimes I even understand what I'm reading about, and it stays in my mind. There are times when I can close my eyes and think of a page and it all comes back like a picture.

Besides history, geography and arithmetic, Miss Kinnian said I should start to learn foreign languages. Dr. Strauss gave me some more tapes to play while I sleep. I still don't understand how that conscious and unconscious mind works, but Dr. Strauss says not to worry yet. He asked me to promise that when I start learning college subjects next week I wouldn't read any books on psychology—that is, until he gives me permission.

I feel a lot better today, but I guess I'm still a little angry that all the time people were laughing and making fun of me because I wasn't so smart. When I become intelligent like Dr. Strauss says, with three times my I.Q. of 68, then maybe I'll be like everyone else and people will like me.

I'm not sure what an I.Q. is. Dr. Nemur said it was something that measured how intelligent you were—like a scale in the drugstore weighs pounds. But Dr. Strauss had a big argument with him and said an I.Q. didn't weigh intelligence at all. He said an I.Q. showed how much intelligence you could get, like the numbers on the outside of a measuring cup. You still had to fill the cup up with stuff.

Then when I asked Burt, who gives me my intelligence tests and works with Algernon, he said that both of them were wrong (only I had to promise not to tell them he said so). Burt says that the I.Q. measures a lot of different things including some of the things you learned already, and it really isn't any good at all.

So I still don't know what I.Q. is except that mine is going to be over 200 soon. I didn't want to say anything, but I don't see how if they don't know *what* it is, or *where* it is—I don't see how they know *how much* of it you've got.

Dr. Nemur says I have to take a *Rorshach* Test tomorrow. I wonder what that is.

April 22 I found out what a Rorshach is. It's the test I took before the operation—the one with the inkblots on the pieces of cardboard.

I was scared to death of those inkblots. I knew the man was going to ask me to find the pictures and I knew I couldn't. I was thinking to myself, if only there was some way of knowing what kind of pictures were hidden there. Maybe there weren't any pictures at all. Maybe it was just a trick to see if I was dumb enough to look for something that wasn't there. Just thinking about that made me sore at him.

"All right, Charlie," he said, "you've seen these cards before, remember?"

"Of course I remember."

The way I said it, he knew I was angry, and he looked surprised. "Yes, of course. Now I want you to look at this. What might this be? What do you see on this card? People see all sorts of things in these inkblots. Tell me what it might be for you—what it makes you think of."

I was shocked. That wasn't what I had expected him to say. "You mean there are no pictures hidden in those inkblots?"

He frowned and took off his glasses. "What?"

"Pictures. Hidden in the inkblots. Last time you told me everyone could see them and you wanted me to find them too."

He explained to me that the last time he had used almost the exact same words he was using now. I didn't believe it, and I still have the suspicion that he misled me at the time just for the fun of it. Unless—I don't know any more— could I have been that feeble-minded?

We went through the cards slowly. One looked like a pair of bats tugging at something. Another one looked like two men fencing with swords. I imagined all sort of things. I guess I got carried away. But I didn't trust him any more, and I kept turning them around, even looking on the back to see if there was anything there I was supposed to catch. While he was making his notes, I peeked out of the corner of my eye to read it. But it was all in code that looked like this:

$$WF + A \quad DdF - Ad\ orig. \quad WF - A$$
$$SF + obj$$

The test still doesn't make sense to me. It seems to me that anyone could make up lies about things that they didn't really imagine. Maybe I'll understand it when Dr. Strauss lets me read up on psychology.

April 25 I figured out a new way to line up the machines in the factory, and Mr. Donnegan says it will save him ten thousand dollars a year in labor and increased production. He gave me a $25 bonus.

I wanted to take Joe Carp and Frank Reilly out to lunch to celebrate, but Joe said he had to buy some things for his wife, and Frank said he was meeting his cousin for lunch. I guess it'll take a little time for them to get used to the changes in me. Everybody seems to be frightened of me. When I went over to Amos Borg and tapped him, he jumped up in the air.

People don't talk to me much any more or kid around the way they used to. It makes the job kind of lonely.

April 27 I got up nerve today to ask Miss Kinnian to have dinner with me tomorrow night to celebrate my bonus.

At first she wasn't sure it was right, but I asked Dr. Strauss and he said it was okay. Dr. Strauss and Dr. Nemur don't seem to be getting along so well. They're arguing all the time. This evening I heard them shouting. Dr. Nemur was saying that it was his experiment and his research, and Dr. Strauss shouted back that he contributed just as much, because he found me through Miss Kinnian and he performed the operation. Dr. Strauss said that someday thousands of neurosurgeons might be using his technique all over the world.

Dr. Nemur wanted to publish the results of the experiment at the end of this month. Dr. Strauss wanted to wait a while to be sure. Dr. Strauss said Dr. Nemur was more interested in the Chair of Psychology at Princeton than he was in the experiment. Dr. Nemur said Dr. Strauss was nothing but an opportunist trying to ride to glory on his coattails.

When I left afterwards I found myself trembling. I don't know why for sure, but it was as if I'd seen both men clearly for the first time. I remember hearing Burt say Dr. Nemur had a shrew of a wife who was pushing him all the time to get things published so he could become famous. Burt said that the dream of her life was to have a big shot husband.

April 28 I don't understand why I never noticed how beautiful Miss Kinnian really is. She has brown eyes and feathery brown hair that comes to the top of her neck. She's only thirty-four! I think from the beginning I had the feeling that she was an unreachable genius—and very, very old. Now, every time I see her she grows younger and more lovely.

We had dinner and a long talk. When she said I was coming along so fast I'd be leaving her behind, I laughed.

"It's true, Charlie. You're already a better reader than I am. You can read a whole page at a glance while I can take in only a few lines at a time. And you remember every single thing you read. I'm lucky if I can recall the main thoughts and the general meaning."

"I don't feel intelligent. There are so many things I don't understand."

She took out a cigarette and I lit it for her. "You've got to be a little patient. You're accomplishing in days and weeks what it takes normal people a lifetime to do. That's what makes it so amazing. You're like a giant sponge now, soaking things in. Facts, figures, general knowledge. And soon you'll begin to connect them too. You'll see how different branches of learning are related. There are many levels, Charlie, like steps on a giant ladder that take you up higher and higher to see more and more of the world around you.

"I can see only a little bit of that, Charlie, and I won't go much higher than I am now, but you'll keep climbing up and up, and see more and more, and each step will open new worlds that you never even knew existed." She frowned. "I hope . . . I just hope to God—"

"What?"

"Never mind, Charlie. I just hope I wasn't wrong to advise you to go into this in the first place."

I laughed. "How could that be? It worked, didn't it? Even Algernon is still smart."

We sat there silently for a while and I knew what she was thinking about as she watched me toying with the chain of my rabbit's foot and my keys. I didn't want to think of that possibility any more than elderly people want to think of death. I knew that this was only the beginning. I knew what she meant about levels because I'd seen some of them already. The thought of leaving her behind made me sad.

I'm in love with Miss Kinnian.

progress report 12

April 30 I've quit my job with Donnegan's Plastic Box Company. Mr. Donnegan insisted it would be better for all concerned if I left. What did I do to make them hate me so?

The first I knew of it was when Mr. Donnegan showed me the petition. Eight hundred names, everyone in the factory, except Fanny Girden. Scanning the list quickly, I saw at once that hers was the only missing name. All the rest demanded that I be fired.

Joe Carp and Frank Reilly wouldn't talk to me about it. No one else would either, except Fanny. She was one of the few people I'd known who set her mind to something and believed it no matter what the rest of the world proved, said, or did—and Fanny did not believe that I should have been fired. She had been against the petition on principle and despite the pressure and threats she'd held out.

"Which don't mean to say," she remarked, "that I don't think there's something mighty strange about you, Charlie. Them changes. I don't know. You used to be a good, dependable, ordinary man—not too bright maybe, but honest. Who knows what you done to yourself to get so smart all of a sudden. Like everybody around here's been saying, Charlie, it's not right."

"But how can you say that, Fanny? What's wrong with a man becoming intelligent and wanting to acquire knowledge and understanding of the world around him?"

She stared down at her work and I turned to leave. Without looking at me, she said: "It was evil when Eve listened to the snake and ate from the tree of knowledge. It was evil when she saw that she was naked. If not for that none of us would ever have to grow old and sick, and die."

Once again now, I have the feeling of shame burning inside me. This intelligence has driven a wedge between me and all the people I once knew and loved. Before, they laughed at me and despised me for my ignorance and dullness; now, they hate me for my knowledge and understanding. What in God's name do they want of me?

They've driven me out of the factory. Now I'm more alone than ever before. . . .

May 15 Dr. Strauss is very angry at me for not having written any progress reports in two weeks. He's justified because the lab is now paying me a regular salary. I told him I was too busy thinking and reading. When I pointed out that writing was such a slow process that it made me impatient with my poor handwriting, he suggested I learn to type. It's much easier to write now because I can type seventy-five words a minute. Dr. Strauss continually reminds me of the need to speak and write simply so people will be able to understand me.

I'll try to review all the things that happened to me during the last two weeks. Algernon and I were presented to the American Psychological Association sitting in convention with the World Psychological Association. We created quite a sensation. Dr. Nemur and Dr. Strauss were proud of us.

I suspect that Dr. Nemur, who is sixty—ten years older than Dr. Strauss—finds it necessary to see tangible results of his work. Undoubtedly the result of pressure by Mrs. Nemur.

Contrary to my earlier impressions of him, I realize that Dr. Nemur is not at all a genius. He has a very good mind, but it struggles under the spectre of self-doubt. He wants people to take him for a genius. Therefore it is important for him to feel that his work is accepted by the world. I believe that Dr. Nemur was afraid of further delay because he worried that someone else might make a discovery along these lines and take the credit from him.

Dr. Strauss on the other hand might be called a genius, although I feel his areas of knowledge are too limited. He was educated in the tradition of narrow specialization; the broader aspects of background were neglected far more than necessary—even for a neurosurgeon.

I was shocked to learn the only ancient languages he could read were Latin, Greek, and Hebrew, and that he knows almost nothing of mathematics beyond the elementary levels of the calculus of variations. When he admitted this to me, I found myself almost annoyed. It was as if he'd hidden this part of himself in

order to deceive me, pretending—as do many
people I've discovered—to be what he is not. No
one I've ever known is what he appears to be
on the surface.

Dr. Nemur appears to be uncomfortable
around me. Sometimes when I try to talk to him
he just looks at me strangely and turns away.

I was angry at first when Dr. Strauss told me
I was giving Dr. Nemur an inferiority complex.
I thought he was mocking me and I'm over-
sensitive at being made fun of.

How was I to know that a highly respected
psycho-experimentalist like Nemur was unac-
quainted with Hindustani and Chinese? It's absurd when you consider the work that is being
done in India and China today in the very field
of his study.

I asked Dr. Strauss how Nemur could refute
Rahajamati's attack on his method if Nemur
couldn't even read it in the first place. That
strange look on Strauss' face can mean only one
of two things. Either he doesn't want to tell
Nemur what they're saying in India, or else—
and this worries me—Dr. Strauss doesn't know
either. I must be careful to speak and write
clearly and simply so people won't laugh.

May 18 I am very disturbed. I saw Miss Kinnian last night for the first time in over a week.
I tried to avoid all discussions of intellectual
concepts and to keep the conversation on a simple, everyday level, but she just stared at me
blankly and asked me what I meant about the
mathematical variance equivalent in Dorber-
mann's *Fifth Concerto*.

When I tried to explain she stopped me and laughed. I guess I got angry, but I suspect I'm approaching her on the wrong level. No matter what I try to discuss with her, I am unable to communicate. I must review Vrostadt's equations on *Levels of Semantic Progression*. I find I don't communicate with people much any more. Thank God for books and music and things I can think about. I am alone at Mrs. Flynn's boardinghouse most of the time and seldom speak to anyone.

May 20 I would not have noticed the new dishwasher, a boy of about sixteen, at the corner diner where I take my evening meals, if not for the incident of the broken dishes.

They crashed to the floor, sending bits of white china under the tables. The boy stood there, dazed and frightened, holding the empty tray in his hand. The catcalls from the customers (the cries of "Hey, there go the profits!" . . . "*Mazeltov!*" . . . and "Well, he didn't work here very long . . ." which invariably seem to follow the breaking of glass or dishware in a public restaurant) all seemed to confuse him.

When the owner came to see what the excitement was about, the boy cowered as if he expected to be struck. "All right! All right, you dope," shouted the owner, "don't just stand there! Get the broom and sweep that mess up. A broom . . . a broom, you idiot! It's in the kitchen!"

The boy saw he was not going to be punished. His frightened expression disappeared and he smiled as he came back with the broom to sweep the floor. A few of the rowdier customers kept up the remarks, amusing themselves at his expense.

"Here, sonny, over here there's a nice piece behind you. . . ."

"He's not so dumb. It's easier to break 'em than wash 'em!"

As his vacant eyes moved across the crowd of onlookers, he slowly mirrored their smiles and finally broke into an uncertain grin at the joke he obviously did not understand.

I felt sick inside as I looked at his dull, vacuous smile, the wide, bright eyes of a child, uncertain but eager to please. They were laughing at him because he was mentally retarded.

And I had been laughing at him too.

Suddenly I was furious at myself and all those who were smirking at him. I jumped up and shouted, "Shut up! Leave him alone! It's not his fault he can't understand! He can't help what he is! But he's still a human being!"

The room grew silent. I cursed myself for losing control. I tried not to look at the boy as I walked out without touching my food. I felt ashamed for both of us.

How strange that people of honest feelings and sensibility, who would not take advantage of a man born without arms or eyes—how such people think nothing of abusing a man born with low intelligence. It infuriated me to think that not too long ago I had foolishly played the clown.

And I had almost forgotten.

I'd hidden the picture of the old Charlie Gordon from myself because now that I was intelligent it was something that had to be pushed out of my mind. But today in looking at that boy, for the first time I saw what I had been. I was just like him!

Only a short time ago, I learned that people laughed at me. Now I can see that unknowingly I joined with them in laughing at myself. That hurts most of all.

I have often reread my progress reports and seen the illiteracy, the childish naïvete, the mind of low intelligence peering from a dark room, through the keyhole at the dazzling light outside. I see that even in my dullness I knew I was inferior, and that other people had something I lacked—something denied me. In my mental blindness, I thought it was somehow connected with the ability to read and write, and I was sure that if I could get those skills I would automatically have intelligence too.

Even a feeble-minded man wants to be like other men.

A child may not know how to feed itself, or what to eat, yet it knows of hunger.

This then is what I was like. I never knew. Even with my gift of intellectual awareness, I never really knew.

This day was good for me. Seeing the past more clearly, I've decided to use my knowledge and skills to work in the field of increasing human intelligence levels. Who is better equipped for this work? Who else has lived in both worlds? These are my people. Let me use my gift to do something for them.

Tomorrow, I will discuss with Dr. Strauss how

I can work in this area. I may be able to help him work out the problems of widespread use of the technique which was used on me. I have several good ideas of my own.

There is so much that might be done with this technique. If I could be made into a genius, what about thousands of others like myself? What fantastic levels might be achieved by using this technique on normal people? On geniuses?

There are so many doors to open. I am impatient to begin.

progress report 13

May 23 It happened today. Algernon bit me. I visited the lab to see him as I do occasionally, and when I took him out of his cage, he snapped at my hand. I put him back and watched him for a while. He was unusually disturbed and vicious.

May 24 Burt, who is in charge of the experimental animals, tells me that Algernon is changing. He is less cooperative; he refuses to run the maze any more; general motivation has decreased. And he hasn't been eating. Everyone is upset about what this may mean.

May 25 They've been feeding Algernon, who now refuses to work the shifting-lock problem. Everyone identifies me with Algernon. In a way we're both the first of our kind. They're all pretending that Algernon's behavior is not necessarily significant for me. But it's hard to hide the fact that some of the other animals who were used in this experiment are showing strange behavior.

Dr. Strauss and Dr. Nemur have asked me not to come to the lab any more. I know what they're thinking but I can't accept it. I am going ahead with my plans to carry their research forward. With all due respect to both these fine scientists, I am well aware of their limitations. If there is an answer, I'll have to find it out for myself. Suddenly, time has become very important to me.

May 29 I have been given a lab of my own and permission to go ahead with the research. I'm onto something. Working day and night. I've had a cot moved into the lab. Most of my writing time is spent on the notes which I keep in a separate folder, but from time to time I feel it necessary to put down my moods and thoughts from sheer habit.

I find the calculus of intelligence to be a fascinating study. Here is the place for the application of all the knowledge I have acquired.

May 31 Dr. Strauss thinks I'm working too hard. Dr. Nemur says I'm trying to cram a lifetime of research and thought into a few weeks. I know I should rest, but I'm driven on by something inside that won't let me stop. I've got to find the reason for the sharp regression in Algernon. I've got to know if and when it will happen to me.

LETTER TO DR. STRAUSS (copy)

Dear Dr. Strauss:

Under separate cover I am sending you a copy of my report entitled, "The Algernon-Gordon Effect: A Study of Structure and Function of Increased Intelligence," which I would like to have published.

As you see, my experiments are completed. I have included in my report all of my formulae, as well as mathematical analysis in the appendix. Of course, these should be verified.

Because of its importance to both you and Dr. Nemur (and need I say to myself, too?) I have checked and rechecked my results a dozen times in the hope of finding an error. I am sorry to say the results must stand. Yet for the sake of science, I am grateful for the little bit that I here add to the knowledge of the function of the human mind and of the laws governing the artificial increase of human intelligence.

I recall your once saying to me that an experimental failure or the disproving of a theory was as important to the advancement of learning as a success would be. I know now that this is true. I am sorry, however, that my own contribution to the field must rest upon the ashes of the work of two men I regard so highly.

Yours truly,
CHARLES GORDON

June 5 I must not become emotional. The facts and the results of my experiments are clear, and the more sensational aspects of my own rapid climb cannot obscure the fact that the tripling of my intelligence by the surgical technique developed by Drs. Strauss and Nemur must be viewed as having little or no practical applicability (at the present time) to the increase of human intelligence.

As I review the records and data on Algernon, I see that although he is still in his physical infancy, he has regressed mentally. Motor activity is impaired; there is a general reduction of glandular activity; there is an accelerated loss of coordination.

There are also strong indications of progressive amnesia.

As will be seen by my report, these and other physical and mental deterioration syndromes can be predicted with significant results by the application of my formula.

The surgical stimulus to which we were both subjected has resulted in an intensification and acceleration of all mental processes. The unforeseen development, which I have taken the liberty of calling the Algernon-Gordon Effect, is the logical extension of the entire intelligence speed-up. The hypothesis here proven may be described simply in the following terms: Artificially increased intelligence deteriorates at a rate of time directly proportional to the quantity of the increase.

I feel that this, in itself, is an important discovery.

As long as I am able to write, I will continue to record my thoughts in these progress reports. It is one of my few pleasures. However, by all indications, my own mental deterioration will be very rapid.

I have already begun to notice signs of emotional instability and forgetfulness, the first symptoms of the burnout.

June 10 Deterioration progressing. I have become absent-minded. Algernon died two days ago. Dissection shows my predictions were right. His brain had decreased in weight and there was a general smoothing out of cerebral convolutions, as well as a deepening and broadening of brain fissures.

I guess the same thing is or will soon be happening in me. Now that it's definite, I don't want it to happen.

I put Algernon's body in a cheese box and buried him in the backyard. I cried.

June 15 Dr. Strauss came to see me again. I wouldn't open the door and I told him to go away. I want to be left to myself. I am touchy and irritable. I feel the darkness closing in. It's hard to throw off thoughts of suicide. I keep telling myself how important this journal will be.

It's a strange sensation to pick up a book you enjoyed just a few months ago and discover you don't remember it. I remembered how great I thought John Milton was, but when I picked up *Paradise Lost* I couldn't understand it at all. I got so angry I threw the book across the room.

I've got to try to hold on to some of it. Some of the things I've learned. Oh, God, please don't take it all away.

June 19 Sometimes, at night, I go out for a walk. Last night, I couldn't remember where I lived. A policeman took me home. I have the strange feeling that this has all happened to me before—a long time ago. I keep telling myself I'm the only person in the world who can describe what's happening to me.

June 21 Why can't I remember? I've got to fight. I lie in bed for days and I don't know who or where I am. Then it all comes back to me in a flash. Fugues of amnesia. Symtoms of senility—second childhood. I can watch them coming on. It's so cruelly logical. I learned so much and so fast. Now my mind is deteriorating rapidly. I won't let it happen. I'll fight it. I can't help thinking of the boy in the restaurant, the blank expression, the silly smile, the people laughing at him. No—please—not that again. . . .

June 22 I'm forgetting things that I learned recently. It seems to be following the classic pattern—the last things learned are the first things forgotten. Or is that the pattern? I'd better look it up again. . . .

I reread my paper on the Algernon-Gordon Effect and I get the strange feeling that it was written by someone else. There are parts I don't even understand.

Motor activity impaired. I keep tripping over

things, and it becomes increasingly difficult to type.

June 23 I've given up using the typewriter. My coordination is bad. I feel I'm moving slower and slower. Had a terrible shock today. I picked up a copy of an article I used in my research, Kreuger's *Uber Psychische Ganzheit,* to see if it would help me understand what I had done. First I thought there was something wrong with my eyes. Then I realized I could no longer read German. I tested myself in other languages. All gone.

June 30 A week since I dared to write again. It's slipping away like sand through my fingers. Most of the books I have are too hard for me now. I get angry with them because I know that I read and understood them just a few weeks ago.

I keep telling myself I must keep writing these reports so that somebody will know what is happening to me. But it gets harder to form the words and remember spellings. I have to look up even simple words in the dictionary now and it makes me impatient with myself.

Dr. Strauss comes around almost every day, but I told him I wouldn't see or speak to anybody. He feels guilty. They all do. But I don't blame anyone. I knew what might happen. But how it hurts.

July 7 I don't know where the week went. Todays Sunday I know because I can see through my window people going to church. I think I stayed in bed all week but I remember Mrs. Flynn bringing food to me a few times. I keep saying over and over I've got to do something but then I forget or maybe its just easier not to do what I say I'm going to do.

I think of my mother and father a lot these days. I found a picture of them with me taken at a beach. My father has a big ball under his arm and my mother is holding me by the hand. I don't remember them the way they are in the picture. All I remember is my father drunk most of the time and arguing with mom about money.

He never shaved much and he used to scratch my face when he hugged me. My mother said he died but Cousin Miltie said he heard his dad say that my father ran away with another woman. When I asked my mother she slapped me and said my father was dead. I dont think I ever found out the truth but I dont care much. (He said he was going to take me to see cows on a farm once but he never did. He never kept his promises. . . .)

July 10 My landlady Mrs. Flynn is very worried about me. She says the way I lay around all day and dont do anything I remind her of her son before she threw him out of the house. She said she doesn't like loafers. If Im sick its one thing, but if Im a loafer thats another thing and she won't have it. I told her I think Im sick.

I try to read a little bit every day, mostly stories, but sometimes I have to read the same thing over and over again because I don't know what it means. And its hard to write. I know I should look up all the words in the dictionary but its so hard and Im so tired all the time.

Then I got the idea that I would only use the easy words instead of the long hard ones. That saves time. I put flowers on Algernons grave about once a week. Mrs. Flynn thinks Im crazy to put flowers on a mouses grave but I told her that Algernon was special.

July 14 Its sunday again. I dont have anything to do to keep me busy now because my television set is broke and I dont have any money to get it fixed. (I think I lost this months check from the lab. I dont remember)

I get awful headaches and asperin doesnt help me much. Mrs. Flynn knows Im really sick and she feels very sorry for me. Shes a wonderful woman whenever someone is sick.

July 22 Mrs. Flynn called a strange doctor to see me. She was afraid I was going to die. I told the doctor I wasnt too sick and I only forget sometimes. He asked me did I have any friends or relatives and I said no I dont have any. I told him I had a friend called Algernon once but he was a mouse and we used to run races together. He looked at me kind of funny like he thought I was crazy. He smiled when I told him I used to be a genius. He talked to me like I was a baby and he winked at Mrs. Flynn. I got mad and chased him out because he was making fun of me the way they all used to.

July 24 I have no more money and Mrs Flynn says I got to go to work somewhere and pay the rent because I havent paid for two months. I dont know any work but the job I used to have at Donnegans Box Company. I dont want to go back because they all knew me when I was smart and maybe they'll laugh at me. But I dont know what else to do to get money.

July 25 I was looking at some of my old progress reports and its very funny but I cant read what I wrote. I can make out some of the words but they dont make sense.

Miss Kinnian came to the door but I said go away I dont want to see you. She cried and I cried too but I wouldnt let her in because I didnt want her to laugh at me. I told her I didnt like her any more. I told her I didnt want to be smart any more. Thats not true. I still love her and I still want to be smart but I had to say that so shed go away. She gave Mrs. Flynn money to pay the rent. I dont want that. I got to get a job.

Please . . . please let me not forget how to read and write. . . .

July 27 Mr. Donnegan was very nice when I came back and asked him for my old job of janitor. First he was very suspicious but I told him what happened to me then he looked very sad and put his hand on my shoulder and said Charlie Gordon you got guts.

Everybody looked at me when I came downstairs and started working in the toilet sweeping it out like I used to. I told myself Charlie if they make fun of you dont get sore because you remember their not so smart as you once thot they were. And besides they were once your friends and if they laughed at you that doesnt mean anything because they liked you too.

One of the new men who came to work there after I went away made a nasty crack he said hey Charlie I hear your a very smart fella a real quiz kid. Say something intelligent. I felt bad but Joe Carp came over and grabbed him by the shirt and said leave him alone you lousy cracker or I'll break your neck. I didnt expect Joe to take my part so I guess hes really my friend.

Later Frank Reilly came over and said Charlie if anybody bothers you or trys to take advantage you call me or Joe and we will set em straight. I said thanks Frank and I got choked up so I had to turn around and go into the supply room so he wouldnt see me cry. Its good to have friends.

July 28 I did a dumb thing today I forgot I wasnt in Miss Kinnians class at the adult center any more like I use to be. I went in and sat down in my old seat in the back of the room and she looked at me funny and she said Charles. I dint remember she ever called me that before only Charlie so I said hello Miss Kinnian Im redy for my lesin today only I lost my reader that we was using. She startid to cry and run out of the room and everybody looked at me and I saw they wasnt the same pepul who use to be in my class.

Then all of a suddin I remembered some things about the operashun and me getting smart and I said holy smoke I reely pulled a Charlie Gordon that time. I went away before she come back to the room.

Thats why Im going away from New York for good. I dont want to do nothing like that agen. I dont want Miss Kinnian to feel sorry for me. Evry body feels sorry at the factery and I dont want that eather so Im going someplace where nobody knows that Charlie Gordon was once a genius and now he cant even reed a book or rite good.

Im taking a cuple of books along and even if I cant reed them Ill practise hard and maybe wont forget every thing I lerned. If I try reel hard maybe Ill be a littel bit smarter than I was before the operashun. I got my rabits foot and my luky penny and maybe they will help me.

If you ever reed this Miss Kinnian dont be sorry for me Im glad I got a second chanse to be smart becaus I lerned a lot of things that I never even new were in this world and Im grateful that I saw it all for a littel bit. I dont know why Im dumb agen or what I did wrong maybe its because I dint try hard enuff. But if I try and practis very hard maybe Ill get a littl smarter and know what all the words are. I remember a littel bit how nice I had a feeling with the blue book that has the torn cover when I red it. Thats why Im gonna keep trying to get smart so I can have that feeling agen. Its a good feeling to know things and be smart. I wish

I had it rite now if I did I would sit down and reed all the time. Anyway I bet Im the first dumb person in the world who ever found out something importent for science. I remember I did somthing but I dont remember what. So I guess its like I did it for all the dumb pepul like me.

Goodbye Miss Kinnian and Dr. Strauss and everybody. And P.S. please tell Dr. Nemur not to be such a grouch when pepul laff at him and he would have more frends. Its easy to make frends if you let pepul laff at you. Im going to have lots of frends where I go.

P.P.S. Please if you get a chanse put some flowrs on Algernons grave in the bak yard. . . .

ONE ORDINARY DAY, WITH PEANUTS

SHIRLEY JACKSON

MR. JOHN PHILIP JOHNSON shut his front door behind him and came down his front steps into the bright morning with a feeling that all was well with the world on this best of all days, and wasn't the sun warm and good, and didn't his shoes feel comfortable after the resoling, and he knew that he had undoubtedly chosen the precise very tie which belonged with the day and the sun and his comfortable feet, and, after all, wasn't the world just a wonderful place? In spite of the fact that he was a small man, and the tie was perhaps a shade vivid, Mr. Johnson irradiated this feeling of well-being as he came down the steps and onto the dirty sidewalk, and he smiled at people who passed him, and some of them even smiled back. He stopped at the newsstand on the corner and bought his paper, saying "*Good* morning" with real conviction to the man who sold him the paper and the two or three other people who were lucky enough to be buying papers when Mr. Johnson skipped up. He remembered to fill his pockets with candy and peanuts, and then he set out to get himself uptown. He stopped in a flower shop and bought a carnation for his buttonhole, and stopped almost immediately afterward to give the carnation to a small child in a carriage, who looked at him dumbly and smiled, and Mr. Johnson smiled, and the child's mother looked at Mr. Johnson for a minute and then smiled too.

When he had gone several blocks uptown, Mr. Johnson cut across the avenue and went along a side street, chosen at random; he did not follow the same route every morning, but preferred to pursue his eventful way in wide detours, more like a puppy than a man intent upon business. It happened this morning that halfway down the block a moving van was parked, and the furniture from an upstairs apartment stood half on the sidewalk, half on the steps, while an amused group of people loitered, examining the scratches on the tables and the worn spots on the chairs, and a harassed woman, trying to watch a young child and the movers and the furniture all at the same time, gave the clear impression of endeavoring to shelter her private life from the people staring at her belongings. Mr. Johnson stopped, and for a moment joined the crowd, and then he came forward and, touching his hat civilly, said, "Perhaps I can keep an eye on your little boy for you?"

The woman turned and glared at him distrustfully, and Mr. Johnson added hastily, "We'll sit right here on the steps." He beckoned to the little boy, who hesitated and then responded agreeably to Mr. Johnson's genial smile. Mr. Johnson brought out a handful of peanuts from his pocket and sat on the steps with the boy, who at first refused the peanuts on the grounds that his mother did not allow him to accept food from strangers; Mr. Johnson said that probably his mother had not intended peanuts to be included, since elephants at the circus ate them, and the boy considered, and then agreed solemnly. They sat on the steps cracking peanuts in a comradely fashion, and Mr. Johnson said, "So you're moving?"

"Yep," said the boy.

"Where you going?"

"Vermont."

"Nice place. Plenty of snow there. Maple sugar too; you like maple sugar?"

"Sure."

"Plenty of maple sugar in Vermont. You going to live on a farm?"

"Going to live with Grandpa."

"Grandpa like peanuts?"

"Sure."

"Ought to take him some," said Mr. Johnson, reaching smoothly into his pocket. "Just you and Mommy going?"

"Yep."

"Tell you what," Mr. Johnson said. "You take some peanuts to eat on the train."

The boy's mother, after glancing at them frequently, had seemingly decided that Mr. Johnson was trustworthy, because she had devoted herself wholeheartedly to seeing that the movers did not—what movers rarely do, but every housewife believes they will—crack a leg from her good table, or set a kitchen chair down on a lamp. Most of the furniture was loaded by now, and she was deep in that nervous stage when she knew there was something she had forgotten to pack—hidden away in the back of a closet somewhere, or left at a neighbor's and forgotten, or on the clothesline—and was trying to remember under stress what it was.

"This all, lady?" the chief mover said, completing her dismay.

Uncertainly, she nodded.

"Want to go on the truck with the furniture, sonny?" the mover asked the boy, and laughed. The boy laughed too and said to Mr. Johnson, "I guess I'll have a good time at Vermont."

"Fine time," said Mr. Johnson, and stood up. "Have one more peanut before you go," he said to the boy.

The boy's mother said to Mr. Johnson, "Thank you so much; it was a great help to me."

"Nothing at all," said Mr. Johnson gallantly. "Where in Vermont are you going?"

The mother looked at the little boy accusingly, as though he had given away a secret of some importance, and said unwillingly, "Greenwich."

"Lovely town," said Mr. Johnson. He took out a card, and wrote a name on the back. "Very good friend of mine lives in Greenwich," he said. "Call on him for anything you need. His wife makes the best doughnuts in town," he added soberly to the little boy.

"Swell," said the little boy.

"Good-bye," said Mr. Johnson.

He went on, stepping happily with his new-shod feet, feeling the warm sun on his back and on the top of his head. Halfway down the block he met a stray dog and fed him a peanut.

At the corner, where another wide avenue faced him, Mr. Johnson decided to go on up-town again. Moving with comparative laziness, he was passed on either side by people hurrying and frowning, and people brushed past him going the other way, clattering along to get somewhere quickly. Mr. Johnson stopped on every corner and waited patiently for the light to change, and he stepped out of the way of anyone who seemed to be in any particular hurry, but one young lady came too fast for him, and crashed wildly into him when he stopped to pat a kitten which had run out onto the sidewalk from an apartment house and was now unable to get back through the rushing feet.

"Excuse me," said the young lady, trying frantically to pick up Mr. Johnson and hurry on at the same time. "Terribly sorry."

The kitten, regardless now of danger, raced back to its home. "Perfectly all right," said Mr. Johnson, adjusting himself carefully. "You seem to be in a hurry."

"Of course I'm in a hurry," said the young lady. "I'm late."

She was extremely cross and the frown be-

tween her eyes seemed well on its way to becoming permanent. She had obviously awakened
late, because she had not spent any extra time
in making herself look pretty, and her dress was
plain and unadorned with collar or brooch, and
her lipstick was noticeably crooked. She tried to
brush past Mr. Johnson, but, risking her suspicious displeasure, he took her arm and said,
"Please wait."

"Look," she said ominously, "I ran into you
and your lawyer can see my lawyer and I will
gladly pay all damages and all inconveniences
suffered therefrom but please this minute let
me go because I am late."

"Late for what?" said Mr. Johnson; he tried his
winning smile on her but it did no more than
keep her, he suspected, from knocking him down
again.

"Late for work," she said between her teeth.
"Late for my employment. I have a job and if
I am late I lose exactly so much an hour and I
cannot really afford what your pleasant conversation is costing me, be it ever so pleasant."

"I'll pay for it," said Mr. Johnson. Now these
were magic words, not necessarily because they
were true, or because she seriously expected Mr.
Johnson to pay for anything, but because Mr.
Johnson's flat statement, obviously innocent of
irony, could not be, coming from Mr. Johnson,
anything but the statement of a responsible and
truthful and respectable man.

"What do you mean?" she asked.

"I said that since I am obviously responsible
for your being late I shall certainly pay for it."

"Don't be silly," she said, and for the first time the frown disappeared. "I wouldn't expect you to pay anything—a few minutes ago I was offering to pay you. Anyway," she added, almost smiling, "it was my fault."

"What happens if you don't go to work?"

She stared. "I don't get paid."

"Precisely," said Mr. Johnson.

"What do you mean, precisely? If I don't show up at the office exactly twenty minutes ago I lose a dollar and eighty cents an hour, or three cents a minute or. . . ." She thought. ". . . About a dime for the time I've spent talking to you."

Mr. Johnson laughed, and finally she laughed, too. "You're late already," he pointed out. "Will you give me another six cents worth?"

"I don't understand why."

"You'll see," Mr. Johnson promised. He led her over to the side of the walk, next to the buildings, and said, "Stand here," and went out into the rush of people going both ways. Selecting and considering, as one who must make a choice involving perhaps whole years of lives, he estimated the people going by. Once he almost moved, and then at the last minute thought better of it and drew back. Finally, from half a block away, he saw what he wanted, and moved out into the center of the traffic to intercept a young man, who was hurrying, and dressed as though he had awakened late, and frowning.

"Oof," said the young man, because Mr. Johnson had thought of no better way to intercept anyone than the one the young woman had unwittingly used upon him. "Where do you think you're going?" the young man demanded from the sidewalk.

"I want to speak to you," said Mr. Johnson ominously.

The young man got up nervously, dusting himself and eyeing Mr. Johnson. "What for?" he said. "What'd I do?"

"That's what bothers me most about people nowadays," Mr. Johnson complained broadly to the people passing. "No matter whether they've done anything or not, they always figure someone's after them. About what you're going to do," he told the young man.

"Listen," said the young man, trying to brush past him, "I'm late, and I don't have any time to listen. Here's a dime, now get going."

"Thank you," said Mr. Johnson, pocketing the dime. "Look," he said, "what happens if you stop running?"

"I'm late," said the young man, still trying to get past Mr. Johnson, who was unexpectedly clinging.

"How much do you make an hour?" Mr. Johnson demanded.

"A Communist, are you?" said the young man. "Now will you please let me—"

"No," said Mr. Johnson insistently, "how much?"

"Two fifty," said the young man. "And now will you—"

"You like adventure?"

The young man stared, and, staring, found himself caught and held by Mr. Johnson's genial smile; he almost smiled back and then repressed it and made an effort to tear away. "I got to hurry," he said.

"Mystery? Like surprises? Unusual and exciting events?"

"You selling something?"

"Sure," said Mr. Johnson. "You want to take a chance?"

The young man hesitated, looked longingly up the avenue toward what might have been his destination and then, when Mr. Johnson said "I'll pay for it" with his own peculiar convincing emphasis, turned and said, "Well, okay. But I got to see it first, what I'm buying."

Mr. Johnson, breathing hard, led the young man over to the side where the girl was standing; she had been watching with interest Mr. Johnson's capture of the young man and now, smiling timidly, she looked at Mr. Johnson as though prepared to be surprised at nothing.

Mr. Johnson reached into his pocket and took out his wallet. "Here," he said, and handed two bills to the girl. "This about equals your day's pay."

"But no," she said, surprised in spite of herself. "I mean, I couldn't."

"Please do not interrupt," Mr. Johnson told her. "And here," he said to the young man, "this will take care of you." The young man accepted the money dazedly, but said, "Probably counterfeit" to the young woman out of the side of his mouth. "Now," Mr. Johnson went on, disregarding the young man, "what is your name, miss?"

"Kent," she said helplessly. "Mildred Kent."

"Fine," said Mr. Johnson. "And you, sir?"

"Arthur Adams," said the young man stiffly.

"Splendid," said Mr. Johnson. "Now, Miss Kent, I would like you to meet Mr. Adams. Mr. Adams, Miss Kent."

Miss Kent stared, wet her lips nervously, made a gesture as though she might run, and said, "How do you do?"

Mr. Adams straightened his shoulders, scowled at Mr. Johnson, made a gesture as though he might run, and said, "How do you do?"

"Now this," said Mr. Johnson, taking several bills from his wallet, "should be enough for the day for both of you. I would suggest, perhaps, Coney Island—although I personally am not fond of the place—or perhaps a nice lunch somewhere, and dancing, or a matinee, or even a movie, although take care to choose a really good one; there are so many bad movies these days. You might," he said, struck with an inspiration, "visit the Bronx Zoo, or the Planetarium. Anywhere, as a matter of fact," he concluded, "that you would like to go. Have a nice time."

As he started to move away, Arthur Adams, breaking from his dumbfounded stare, said, "But look here, mister, you can't do this. Why—how do you know—I mean, we don't even know—I mean, how do you know we won't just take the money and not do what you said?"

"You've taken the money," Mr. Johnson said. "You don't have to follow any of my suggestions. You may know something you prefer to do— perhaps a museum, or something."

"But suppose I just run away with it and leave her here?"

"I know you won't," said Mr. Johnson gently, "because you remembered to ask me that. Goodbye," he added, and went on.

As he stepped up the street, conscious of the sun on his head and his good shoes, he heard from somewhere behind him the young man saying, "Look, you know you don't have to if you don't want to," and the girl saying, "But unless you don't want to . . ." Mr. Johnson smiled to himself and then thought that he better hurry along; when he wanted to he could move very quickly, and before the young woman had gotten around to saying, "Well, I will if you will," Mr. Johnson was several blocks away and had already stopped twice, once to help a lady lift several large packages into a taxi and once to hand a peanut to a sea gull. By this time he was in an area of large stores and many more people and he was buffeted constantly from either side by people hurrying and cross and late and sullen. Once he offered a peanut to a man who asked him for a dime, and once he offered a peanut to a bus driver who had stopped his bus at an intersection and had opened the window next to his seat and put out his head as though longing for fresh air and the comparative quiet of the traffic. The man wanting a dime took the peanut because Mr. Johnson had wrapped a dollar bill around it, but the bus driver took the peanut and asked ironically, "You want a transfer, Jack?"

On a busy corner Mr. Johnson encountered two young people—for one minute he thought they might be Mildred Kent and Arthur Adams

—who were eagerly scanning a newspaper, their backs pressed against a storefront to avoid the people passing, their heads bent together. Mr. Johnson, whose curiosity was insatiable, leaned onto the storefront next to them and peeked over the man's shoulder; they were scanning the "Apartments Vacant" columns.

Mr. Johnson remembered the street where the woman and her little boy were going to Vermont and he tapped the man on the shoulder and said amiably, "Try down on West Seventeen. About the middle of the block, people moved out this morning."

"Say, what do you—" said the man, and then, seeing Mr. Johnson clearly, "Well, thanks. Where did you say?"

"West Seventeen," said Mr. Johnson. "About the middle of the block." He smiled again and said, "Good luck."

"Thanks," said the man.

"Thanks," said the girl, as they moved off.

"Good-bye," said Mr. Johnson.

He lunched alone in a pleasant restaurant, where the food was rich, and only Mr. Johnson's excellent digestion could encompass two whipped-cream-and-chocolate-and-rum-cake pastries for desert. He had three cups of coffee, tipped the waiter largely, and went out into the street again into the wonderful sunlight, his shoes still comfortable and fresh on his feet. Outside he found a beggar staring into the windows of the restaurant he had left and, carefully looking through the money in his pocket, Mr. Johnson approached the beggar and pressed some coins and a couple of bills into his hand. "It's the price of the veal cutlet lunch plus tip," said Mr. Johnson. "Good-bye."

After his lunch he rested; he walked into the nearest park and fed peanuts to the pigeons. It was late afternoon by the time he was ready to start back downtown, and he had refereed two checker games and watched a small boy and girl whose mother had fallen asleep and awakened with surprise and fear which turned to amusement when she saw Mr. Johnson. He had given away almost all of his candy, and had fed all the rest of his peanuts to the pigeons, and it was time to go home. Although the late afternoon sun was pleasant, and his shoes were still entirely comfortable, he decided to take a taxi downtown.

He had a difficult time catching a taxi, because he gave up the first three or four empty ones to people who seemed to need them more; finally, however, he stood alone on the corner and—almost like netting a frisky fish—he hailed desperately until he succeeded in catching a cab which had been proceeding with haste uptown and seemed to draw in toward Mr. Johnson against its own will.

"Mister," the cab driver said as Mr. Johnson climbed in, "I figured you was an omen, like. I wasn't going to pick you up at all."

"Kind of you," said Mr. Johnson ambiguously.

"If I'd of let you go it would of cost me ten bucks," said the driver.

"Really?"

"Yeah," said the driver. "Guy just got out of

the cab, he turned around and give me ten bucks, said take this and bet it in a hurry on a horse named Vulcan, right away."

"Vulcan?" said Mr. Johnson, horrified. "A fire sign on a Wednesday?"

"What?" said the driver. "Anyway, I said to myself if I got no fare between here and there I'd bet the ten, but if anyone looked like they needed the cab I'd take it as a omen and I'd take the ten home to the wife."

"You were very right," said Mr. Johnson heartily. "This is Wednesday, you would have lost your money. Monday, yes, or even Saturday. But never never never a fire sign on a Wednesday. Sunday would have been good, now."

"Vulcan don't run on Sunday," said the driver.

"You wait till another day," said Mr. Johnson. "Down this street, please, driver. I'll get off on the next corner."

"He TOLD me Vulcan, though," said the driver.

"I'll tell you," said Mr. Johnson, hesitating with the door of the cab half open. "You take that ten dollars and I'll give you another ten dollars to go with it, and you go right ahead and bet that money on any Thursday on any horse that has a name indicating . . . let me see, Thursday . . . well, grain. Or any growing food."

"Grain?" said the driver. "You mean a horse named, like, Wheat or something?"

"Certainly," said Mr. Johnson. "Or, as a matter of fact, to make it even easier, any horse whose name includes the letters C, R, L. Perfectly simple."

"Tall corn?" said the driver, a light in his eye. "You mean a horse named, like, Tall Corn?"

"Absolutely," said Mr. Johnson. "Here's your money."

"Tall Corn," said the driver. "Thank *you*, mister."

"Good-bye," said Mr. Johnson.

He was on his own corner and went straight up to his apartment. He let himself in and called "Hello?" and Mrs. Johnson answered from the kitchen, "Hello, dear, aren't you early?"

"Took a taxi home," Mr. Johnson said. "I remembered the cheesecake too. What's for dinner?"

Mrs. Johnson came out of the kitchen and kissed him; she was a comfortable woman, and smiling as Mr. Johnson smiled. "Hard day?" she asked.

"Not very," said Mr. Johnson, hanging his coat in the closet. "How about you?"

"So-so," she said. She stood in the kitchen doorway while he settled into his easy chair and took off his good shoes and took out the paper he had bought that morning. "Here and there," she said.

"I didn't do so badly," Mr. Johnson said. "Couple young people."

"Fine," she said. "I had a little nap this afternoon, took it easy most of the day. Went into a department store this morning and accused the woman next to me of shoplifting, and had the store detective pick her up. Sent three dogs to the pound—*you* know, the usual thing. Oh, and listen," she added, remembering.

"What?" asked Mr. Johnson.

"Well," she said, "I got onto a bus and asked the driver for a transfer, and when he helped someone else first I said that he was impertinent, and quarreled with him. And then I said why wasn't he in the army, and I said it loud enough for everyone to hear, and I took his number and I turned in a complaint. Probably got him fired."

"Fine," said Mr. Johnson. "But you do look tired. Want to change over tomorrow?"

"I *would* like to," she said. "I could do with a change."

"Right," said Mr. Johnson. "What's for dinner?"

"Veal cutlet."

"Had it for lunch," said Mr. Johnson.

THE MOST DANGEROUS GAME

RICHARD CONNELL

"OFF THERE TO THE RIGHT—somewhere—is a large island," said Whitney. "It's rather a mystery."

"What island is it?" Rainsford asked.

"The old charts call it 'Ship Trap Island,'" Whitney replied. "A suggestive name, isn't it? Sailors have a curious dread of the place. I don't know why. Some superstition—"

"Can't see it," remarked Rainsford, trying to peer through the dark tropical night that was palpable as it pressed its thick, warm blackness in upon the yacht.

"You have good eyes," said Whitney, with a laugh, "and I've seen you pick off a moose moving in the brown fall bush at four hundred yards; but even you can't see four miles or so through a moonless Caribbean night."

"Nor four yards," admitted Rainsford. "Ugh! It's like moist black velvet."

"It will be light enough in Rio," promised Whitney. "We should make it in a few days. I hope the jaguar guns have come. We'll have some good hunting up the Amazon. Great sport, hunting."

"The best sport in the world," agreed Rainsford.

"For the hunter," amended Whitney. "Not for the jaguar."

"Don't talk rot, Whitney," said Rainsford. "You're a big-game hunter, not a philosopher. Who cares how a jaguar feels?"

"Perhaps the jaguar does," observed Whitney.

"Bah! They've no understanding."

"Even so, I rather think they understand one thing—fear. The fear of pain and the fear of death."

"Nonsense," laughed Rainsford. "This hot weather is making you soft, Whitney. Be a realist. The world is made up of two classes—the hunters and the hunted. Luckily, you and I are hunters. Do you think we've passed that island yet?"

"I can't tell in the dark. I hope so."

"Why?" asked Rainsford.

"The place has a reputation—a bad one. It's gotten into sailor lore, somehow. Didn't you notice that the crew's nerves seemed a bit jumpy today?"

"They were a bit strange, now you mention it. Even Captain Nielson—"

"Yes, even that tough-minded old Swede,

who'd go up to the devil himself and ask him for a light. All I could get out of him was: 'This place has an evil name among seafaring men, sir.' Then he said to me, very gravely: 'Don't you feel anything?'—as if the air about us was actually poisonous. Now, you mustn't laugh when I tell you this—I did feel something like a sudden chill.

"There was no breeze. The sea was as flat as a plate-glass window. We were drawing near the island then. What I felt was a—a mental chill; a sort of sudden dread."

"Pure imagination," said Rainsford. "One superstitious sailor can taint the whole ship's company with his fear."

"Maybe. But sometimes I think sailors have an extra sense that tells them when they are in danger. Sometimes I think evil is a tangible thing—with wave lengths, just as sound and light have. An evil place can, so to speak, broadcast vibrations of evil. Anyhow, I'm glad we're getting out of this zone. Well, I think I'll turn in now, Rainsford."

"I'm not sleepy," said Rainsford. "I'm going to smoke another pipe up on the afterdeck."

"Good night, then. See you at breakfast."

"Right. Good night, Whitney."

Rainsford, reclining in a steamer chair, indolently puffed on his favorite briar. The sensuous drowsiness of the night was on him. "It's so dark," he thought, "that I could sleep without closing my eyes."

An abrupt sound startled him. Off to the right he heard it, and his ears, expert in such matters, could not be mistaken. Again he heard the sound, and again. Somewhere, off in the blackness, someone had fired a gun three times.

Rainsford sprang up and moved quickly to the rail, mystified. He strained his eyes in the direction from which the reports had come, but it was like trying to see through a blanket. He leaped up on the rail and balanced himself there, to get greater elevation; his pipe, striking a rope, was knocked from his mouth. He lunged for it; a short, hoarse cry came from his lips as he realized he had reached too far and had lost his balance. The cry was pinched off short as the blood-warm waters of the Caribbean Sea closed over his head.

He struggled up to the surface and tried to cry out, but the wash from the speeding yacht made him gag and strangle. Desperately he struck out with strong strokes after the receding lights of the yacht, but he stopped before he had swum fifty feet. A certain coolheadedness had come to him; it was not the first time he had been in a tight place. There was a chance that his cries could be heard by someone aboard the yacht, but that chance was slender, and grew more slender as the yacht raced on. He wrestled himself out of his clothes, and shouted with all his power. The lights of the yacht became faint as ever-vanishing fireflies; then they were blotted out entirely by the night.

Rainsford remembered the shots had come from the right; doggedly he swam in that direction, swimming with slow, deliberate strokes, conserving his strength. For a seemingly endless time he fought the sea. He began to count his strokes; he could do possibly a hundred more and then—

Rainsford heard a sound. It came out of the darkness, a high, screaming sound, the sound of an animal in an extremity of anguish and terror.

He did not recognize the animal that made the sound; he did not try to; with fresh vitality he swam toward the sound. He heard it again; then it was cut short by another noise, crisp, staccato.

"Pistol shot," he muttered, swimming on.

Ten minutes of determined effort brought another sound to his ears—the most welcome he had heard—the muttering and growling of the sea breaking on a rocky shore. He was almost on the rocks before he saw them. With his remaining strength he dragged himself from the swirling waters. Jagged crags appeared to jut up into the opaqueness; he forced himself upward, hand over hand. Grasping, his hands raw, he reached a flat place at the top. Dense jungle came down to the very edge of the cliffs. What perils that tangle of trees and underbrush might hold for him did not concern Rainsford just then. All he knew was that he was safe from the sea, and utter weariness was on him. He flung himself down and tumbled headlong into the deepest sleep of his life.

When he opened his eyes, he knew from the position of the sun that it was late in the afternoon. Sleep had given him new vigor; a sharp hunger was picking at him. He looked about him, almost cheerfully.

"Where there are pistol shots, there are men.

Where there are men, there is food," he thought. But what kind of men, he wondered, in so forbidding a place? An unbroken front of snarled and ragged jungle fringed the shore. He saw no sign of a trail through the closely knit web of weeds and trees; it was easier to go along the shore, and he floundered along by the water. Not far from where he had landed, he stopped.

Some wounded thing, by the evidence a large animal, had thrashed about in the underbrush; the jungle weeds were crushed down and the moss was lacerated; one patch of weeds was stained crimson. A small, glittering object not far away caught Rainsford's eye and he picked it up. It was an empty cartridge.

"A twenty-two," he thought. "That's odd. It must have been a fairly large animal too. The hunter had nerve to tackle it with a light gun. It's clear that it put up a fight. I suppose the first three shots I heard were when the hunter flushed his quarry and wounded it. The last shot was when he trailed it here and finished it."

He examined the ground closely and found what he had hoped to find—the print of hunting boots. They pointed along the cliff in the direction he had been going. Eagerly he hurried along, now slipping on a rotten log or a loose stone, but making headway; night was beginning to settle down.

Bleak darkness was blacking out the sea and jungle when Rainsford sighted the lights. He came upon them as he turned a crook in the coast line, and his first thought was that he had come upon a village, for there were many lights.

But as he forged along he saw to his great astonishment that all the lights were in one enormous building—a lofty structure with pointed towers plunging upward into the gloom. His eyes made out the shadowy outlines of a palatial chateau; it was set on a high bluff, and on three sides of it cliffs dived down to where the sea licked greedy lips in the shadows.

"Mirage," thought Rainsford. But it was no mirage, he found, when he opened the tall spiked iron gate. The stone steps were real enough; the massive door with a leering gargoyle for a knocker was real enough; yet about it all hung an air of unreality.

He lifted the knocker; and it creaked stiffly, as if it had never before been used. He let it fall, and it startled him with its booming loudness. He thought he heard steps within; the door remained closed. Again Rainsford lifted the heavy knocker, and let it fall. The door opened suddenly, and Rainsford stood blinking in the river of glaring gold light that poured out. The first thing his eyes discerned was the largest man he had ever seen—a gigantic creature, solidly made and black-bearded almost to the waist. In his hand the man held a long-barreled revolver, and he was pointing it straight at Rainsford's heart. Out of the snarl of beard two small eyes regarded Rainsford.

"Don't be alarmed," said Rainsford, with a smile which he hoped was disarming. "I'm no robber. I fell off a yacht. My name is Sanger Rainsford."

The menacing look in the eyes did not change.

The revolver pointed as rigidly as if the giant were a statue. He gave no sign that he understood Rainsford's words, or that he had even heard them. He was dressed in uniform, a black uniform trimmed with gray astrakhan.

"I'm Sanger Rainsford of New York," Rainsford began again. "I fell off a yacht. I am hungry."

The man's only answer was to raise with his thumb the hammer of his revolver. Then Rainsford saw the man's free hand go to his forehead in a military salute, and he saw him click his heels together and stand at attention. Another man was coming down the broad marble steps, an erect, slender man in evening clothes. He advanced to Rainsford and held out his hand.

In a cultivated voice marked by a slight accent that gave it added precision and deliberateness, he said: "It is a very great pleasure and honor to welcome Mr. Sanger Rainsford, the celebrated hunter, to my home."

Automatically Rainsford shook the man's hand.

"I've read your book about hunting snow leopards in Tibet, you see," explained the man. "I am General Zaroff."

Rainsford's first impression was that the man was singularly handsome; his second was that there was an original, almost bizarre quality about the general's face. He was a tall man past middle age, for his hair was a vivid white; but his thick eyebrows and pointed military mustache were as black as the night. His eyes, too, were black and very bright. He had high cheekbones, a sharp-cut nose, a spare, dark face of an aristocrat. Turning to the giant in uniform, the general made a sign. The giant put away his pistol, saluted, withdrew.

"Ivan is an incredibly strong fellow," remarked the general, "but he has the misfortune to be deaf and dumb. A simple fellow, but I'm afraid, like all his race, a bit of a savage."

"Is he Russian?"

"He is a Cossack," said the general, and his smile showed red lips and pointed teeth. "So am I.

"Come," he said, "we shouldn't be chatting here. We can talk later. Now you want clothes, food, rest. You shall have them. This is a most restful spot."

Ivan had reappeared, and the general spoke to him with lips that moved but gave forth no sound.

"Follow Ivan, if you please, Mr. Rainsford," said the general. "I was about to have my dinner. I'll wait for you. You'll find that my clothes will fit you, I think."

It was to a huge, beam-ceilinged bedroom with a canopied bed big enough for six men that Rainsford followed the silent giant. Ivan laid out an evening suit, and Rainsford put it on.

The dining room to which Ivan conducted him was in many ways remarkable. There was a medieval magnificence about it; it suggested a baronial hall of feudal times with its oaken panels, its high ceiling, its vast refectory table where twoscore men could sit down to eat. About the hall were the mounted heads of many animals —lions, tigers, elephants, moose, beasts; larger or more perfect specimens Rainsford had never seen. At the great table the general was sitting alone. Rainsford noted the table appointments were of the finest—the linen, the crystal, the silver, the china.

They were eating *borsch*. Half apologetically General Zaroff said: "We do our best to preserve the amenities of civilization here. Please forgive any lapses. We are well off the beaten track, you know."

Rainsford was finding the general a most thoughtful and affable host, a true cosmopolite. But there was one small trait of the general's that made Rainsford uncomfortable. Whenever he looked up from his plate he found the general studying him, appraising him narrowly.

"Perhaps," said General Zaroff, "you were surprised that I recognized your name. You see, I read all books on hunting published in English, French, and Russian. I have but one passion in my life, Mr. Rainsford, and that is the hunt."

"You have some wonderful heads here," said Rainsford as he ate a particularly well-cooked filet mignon. "That Cape buffalo is the largest I ever saw."

"Oh, that fellow. Yes, he was a monster."

"Did he charge you?"

"Hurled me against a tree," said the general. "Fractured my skull. But I got the brute."

"I've always thought," said Rainsford, "that the Cape buffalo is the most dangerous of all big game."

For a moment the general did not reply; he was smiling his curious red-lipped smile. Then he said slowly: "No. You are wrong, sir. The Cape buffalo is not the most dangerous big

game." He sipped his wine. "Here in my preserve on this island," he said in the same slow
tone, "I hunt more dangerous game."

Rainsford expressed his surprise. "Is there big
game on this island?"

The general nodded. "The biggest."

"Really?"

"Oh, it isn't here naturally, of course. I have
to stock the island."

"What have you imported, General?" Rainsford asked. "Tigers?"

The general smiled. "No," he said. "Hunting
tigers ceased to interest me years ago. I exhausted their possibilities, you see. No thrill left
in tigers, no real danger. I live for danger, Mr.
Rainsford."

The general took from his pocket a gold cigarette case and offered his guest a long black
cigarette with a silver tip; it was perfumed and
gave off a smell like incense.

"We will have some capital hunting, you and
I," said the general. "I shall be most glad to
have your society."

"But what game—" began Rainsford.

"I'll tell you," said the general. "You will be
amused, I know. I think I may say, in all modesty,
that I have done a rare thing. I have invented a
new sensation. May I pour you another glass of
port, Mr. Rainsford?"

"Thank you, General."

The general filled both glasses, and said: "God
makes some men poets. Some he makes kings,
some beggars. Me He made a hunter. My hand
was made for the trigger, my father said. He

was a very rich man with a quarter of a million acres in the Crimea, and he was an ardent sportsman. When I was only five years old, he gave me a little gun to shoot sparrows with. When I shot some of his prize turkeys with it, he did not punish me; he complimented me on my marksmanship. I killed my first bear when I was ten. My whole life has been one prolonged hunt. I went into the army—it was expected of noblemen's sons—and for a time commanded a division of Cossack cavalry, but my real interest was always the hunt. I have hunted every kind of game in every land. It would be impossible for me to tell you how many animals I have killed."

The general puffed at his cigarette.

"After the debacle in Russia I left the country, for it was imprudent for an officer of the Czar to stay there. Many noble Russians lost everything. I, luckily, had invested heavily in American securities. Naturally, I continued to hunt—grizzlies in your Rockies, crocodiles in the Ganges, rhinoceroses in East Africa. It was in Africa that the Cape buffalo hit me and laid me up for six months. As soon as I recovered I started for the Amazon to hunt jaguars, for I had heard they were unusually cunning. They weren't." The Cossack sighed. "I was bitterly disappointed. I was lying in my tent with a splitting headache one night when a terrible thought pushed its way into my mind. Hunting was beginning to bore me! And hunting, remember, had been my life. I have heard that in America businessmen often go to pieces when they give up the business that has been their life."

172 • NIGHT IN FUNLAND

"Yes, that's so," said Rainsford.

The general smiled. "I had no wish to go to pieces," he said. "I must do something. Now, mine is an analytical mind, Mr. Rainsford. Doubtless that is why I enjoy the problems of the chase."

"No doubt, General Zaroff."

"So," continued the general, "I asked myself why the hunt no longer fascinated me. You are much younger than I am, Mr. Rainsford, and have not hunted as much; but you perhaps can guess the answer."

"What was it?"

"Simply this: Hunting had ceased to be what you call 'a sporting proposition.' It had become too easy. I always got my quarry. Always. There is no greater bore than perfection."

The general lit a fresh cigarette.

"No animal had a chance with me any more. That is no boast; it is a mathematical certainty. The animal had nothing but his legs and his instinct. Instinct is no match for reason. When I thought of this it was a tragic moment for me, I can tell you."

Rainsford leaned across the table, absorbed in what his host was saying.

"It came to me as an inspiration what I must do," the general went on.

"And that was?"

The general smiled the quiet smile of one who has faced an obstacle and surmounted it with success. "I had to invent a new animal to hunt," he said.

"A new animal? You're joking?"

"Not at all," said the general. "I never joke about hunting. I needed a new animal. I found one. So I bought this island, built this house, and here I do my hunting. The island is perfect for my purposes—there are jungles with a maze of trails in them, hills, swamps—"

"But the animal, General Zaroff?"

"Oh," said the general, "it supplies me with the most exciting hunting in the world. No other hunting compares with it for an instant. Every day I hunt, and I never grow bored now, for I have a quarry with which I can match my wits."

Rainsford's bewilderment showed in his face. "I wanted the ideal animal to hunt," explained the general. "So I said: 'What are the attributes of an ideal quarry?' And the answer was, of course: 'It must have courage, cunning, and above all, it must be able to reason.'"

"But no animal can reason," objected Rainsford.

"My dear fellow," said the general, "there is one that can."

"But you can't mean—" gasped Rainsford.

"And why not?"

"I can't believe you are serious, General Zaroff. This is a grisly joke."

"Why should I not be serious? I am speaking of hunting."

The general laughed with entire good nature. He regarded Rainsford quizzically. "I refuse to believe that so modern and civilized a young man as you seem to be harbors romantic ideas about the value of human life. Surely your experience in the war—"

"Did not make me condone cold-blooded murder," finished Rainsford stiffly.

Laughter shook the general. "How extraordinarily droll you are!" he said. "One does not expect nowadays to find a young man of the educated class, even in America, with such a naïve, and, if I may say so, mid-Victorian point of view. Ah, well, I'll wager you'll forget your notions when you go hunting with me. You've a genuine new thrill in store for you, Mr. Rainsford."

"Thank you, I'm a hunter, not a murderer."

"Dear me," said the general, quite unruffled, "again that unpleasant word. But I think I can show you that your scruples are quite ill-founded."

"Yes?"

"Life is for the strong, to be lived by the strong, and, if needs be, taken by the strong. The weak of the world were put here to give the strong pleasure. I am strong. Why should I not use my gift? I wish to hunt, why should I not? I hunt the scum of the earth—sailors from tramp ships—lascars, blacks, Chinese, whites, mongrels—a thoroughbred horse or hound is worth more than a score of them."

"But they are men," said Rainsford hotly.

"Precisely," said the general. "That is why I use them. It gives me pleasure. They can reason, after a fashion. So they are dangerous."

"But where do you get them?"

The general's left eyelid fluttered down in a wink. "This island is called Ship-Trap," he answered. "Sometimes an angry god of the high seas sends them to me. Sometimes, when Providence is not so kind, I help Providence a bit. Come to the window with me."

Rainsford went to the window and looked out toward the sea.

"Watch! Out there!" exclaimed the general, pointing into the night. Rainsford's eyes saw only blackness, and then, as the general pressed a button, far out to sea Rainsford saw the flash of lights.

The general chuckled. "They indicate a channel," he said, "where there's none: giant rocks with razor edges crouch like a sea monster with wide-open jaws. They can crush a ship as easily as I crush this nut." He dropped a walnut on the hardwood floor and brought his heel grinding down on it. "Oh, yes," he said casually, as if in an answer to a question, "I have electricity. We try to be civilized here."

"Civilized? And you shoot down men?"

A trace of anger was in the general's black eyes, but it was there for only a second; then he said, in his most pleasant manner: "Dear me, what a righteous young man you are! I assure you I do not do the thing you suggest. That would be barbarous. I treat these visitors with every consideration. They get plenty of good food and exercise. They get into splendid physical condition. You shall see for yourself tomorrow."

"What do you mean?"

"We shall visit my training school," smiled the general. "It's in the cellar. I have about a dozen pupils down there now. They're from the Spanish bark *San Lucar* that had the bad luck to go on the rocks out there. A very inferior lot, I regret to say. Poor specimens and more accustomed to the deck than the jungle."

He raised his hand, and Ivan brought thick Turkish coffee. Rainsford, with an effort, held his tongue in check.

"It's a game, you see," pursued the general blandly. "I suggest to one of them that we go hunting. I give him a supply of food and an excellent hunting knife. I give him three hours' start. I am to follow, armed only with a pistol of the smallest caliber and range. If my quarry eludes me for three whole days, he wins the game. If I find him"—the general smiles—"he loses."

"Suppose he refused to be hunted?"

"Oh," said the general, "I give him his option, of course. He need not play that game if he doesn't wish to. If he does not wish to hunt, I turn him over to Ivan. Ivan once had the honor of serving as official flogger to the Great White Czar, and he has his own ideas of sport. Invariably, Mr. Rainsford, invariably they choose the hunt."

"And if they win?"

The smile on the general's face widened. "To date I have not lost," he said.

Then he added, hastily: "I don't wish you to think me a braggart, Mr. Rainsford. Many of them afford only the most elementary sort of problem. Occasionally I strike a tartar. One almost did win. I eventually had to use the dogs."

"The dogs?"

"This way, please. I'll show you."

The general steered Rainsford to a window. The lights from the windows sent a flickering illumination that made grotesque patterns on the courtyard below, and Rainsford could see moving shapes; as they turned toward him, their eyes glittered greenly.

"A rather good lot, I think," observed the general. "They are let out at seven every night. If anyone should try to get into my house—or out of it—something extremely regrettable would occur to him." He hummed a snatch of a gay French song.

"And now," said the general, "I want to show you my new collection of heads. Will you come with me to the library?"

"I hope," said Rainsford, "that you will excuse me tonight, General Zaroff. I'm really not feeling at all well."

"Ah, indeed?" the general inquired solicitously. "Well, I suppose that's only natural after your long swim. You need a good, restful night's sleep. Tomorrow you'll feel like a new man, I'll wager. Then we'll hunt, eh? I've one rather promising prospect—"

Rainsford was hurrying from the room.

"Sorry you can't go with me tonight," called the general. "I expect rather fair sport—a big, strong one. He looks resourceful—well, good night, Mr. Rainsford; I hope you have a good night's rest."

The bed was good, and the pajamas of the softest silk, and he was tired in every fiber of his being; nevertheless Rainsford could not quiet his brain with the opiate of sleep. He lay, eyes wide open. Once he thought he heard stealthy steps in the corridor outside his room. He sought to throw open the door; it would not open. He went to the window and looked out. His room was high up in one of the towers. The lights of the chateau were out now, and it was dark and silent, but there was a fragment of sallow moon, and by its wan light he could see, dimly, the courtyard; there, weaving in and out in the pattern of shadow, were black, noiseless forms; the hounds heard him at the window and looked up, expectantly, with their green eyes. Rainsford went back to the bed and lay down. By many methods he tried to put himself to sleep. He had achieved a doze when, just as morning began to come, he heard far off in the jungle, the faint report of a pistol.

General Zaroff did not appear until luncheon. He was dressed faultlessly in the tweeds of a country squire. He was solicitous about the state of Rainsford's health.

"As for me," sighed the general, "I do not feel so well. I am worried, Mr. Rainsford. Last night I detected traces of my old complaint."

To Rainsford's questioning glance the general said: "Ennui. Boredom."

Then, taking a second helping of crepes suzette, the general explained: "The hunting was not good last night. The fellow lost his head. He made a straight trail that offered no problems at all. That's the trouble with these sailors; they have dull brains to begin with, and they do not know how to get about in the woods. They do excessively stupid and obvious things. It's most annoying. Will you have another glass of wine, Mr. Rainsford?"

"General," said Rainsford firmly, "I wish to leave this island at once."

The general raised his eyebrows; he seemed hurt. "But, my dear fellow," he protested, "you've only just come. You've had no hunting—"

"I wish to go today," said Rainsford. He saw the dead-black eyes of the general on him, studying him. General Zaroff's face suddenly brightened.

He filled Rainsford's glass from a dusty bottle.

"Tonight," said the general, "we will hunt—you and I."

Rainsford shook his head. "No, General," he said. "I will not hunt."

The general shrugged his shoulders and delicately ate a hothouse grape. "As you wish, my friend," he said. "The choice rests entirely with you. But may I not venture to suggest that you will find my idea of sport more diverting than Ivan's?"

He nodded toward the corner to where the giant stood, scowling, his thick arms crossed on his chest.

"You don't mean—" Rainsford gasped.

"My dear fellow," said the general, "have I not told you I always mean what I say about hunting? This is really an inspiration. I drink to a foeman worthy of my steel—at last."

The general raised his glass, but Rainsford sat staring at him.

"You'll find this game worth playing," the general said enthusiastically. "Your brain against mine. Your woodcraft against mine. Your strength and stamina against mine. Outdoor chess! And the stake is not without value, eh?"

"And if I win—" began Rainsford huskily.

"I'll cheerfully acknowledge myself defeated if I do not find you by midnight of the third day," said General Zaroff. "My sloop will place you on the mainland near a town."

The general read what Rainsford was thinking.

"Oh, you can trust me," said the Cossack. "I will give you my word as a gentleman and a sportsman. Of course, you in turn must agree to say nothing of your visit here."

"I'll agree to nothing of the kind," said Rainsford.

"Oh," said the general, "in that case—But why discuss that now? Three days hence we can discuss it over a bottle of wine, unless—"

The general sipped his port.

Then a businesslike air animated him. "Ivan," he said to Rainsford, "will supply you with hunting clothes, food, a knife. I suggest you wear moccasins; they leave a poorer trail. I suggest, too, that you avoid the big swamp in the southeast corner of the island. We call it Death Swamp. There's quicksand there. One foolish fellow tried it. The deplorable part of it was that Lazarus followed him. You can imagine my feelings, Mr. Rainsford. I loved Lazarus; he was the finest hound in my pack. Well, I must beg you to excuse me now. I always take a siesta after lunch. You'll hardly have time for a nap, I fear. You'll want to start, no doubt. I shall not follow till dusk. Hunting at night is so much more exciting than by day, don't you think? *Au revoir*, Mr. Rainsford, *au revoir*."

General Zaroff, with a deep, courtly bow, strolled from the room. From another door came

Ivan. Under one arm he carried khaki hunting clothes, a haversack of food, a leather sheath containing a long-bladed hunting knife; his right hand rested on a cocked revolver thrust in the crimson sash about his waist. . . .

Rainsford had fought his way through the bush for two hours. "I must keep my nerve," he thought tensely.

He had not been entirely clear-headed when the chateau gates snapped shut behind him. His whole idea at first was to put distance between himself and General Zaroff; and, to this end, he had plunged along, spurred on by something very much like panic. Now he had got a grip on himself, had stopped, and was taking stock of himself and the situation.

He saw that straight flight was futile; inevitably it would bring him face to face with the sea. He was in a picture with a frame of water, and his operations, clearly, must take place within that frame.

"I'll give him a trail to follow," muttered Rainsford, and he struck off from the rude path he had been following into the trackless wilderness. He executed a series of intricate loops; he doubled on his trail again and again, recalling all the lore of the fox hunt, and all the dodges of the fox. Night found him leg-weary, with hands and face lashed by the branches, on a thickly wooded ridge. He knew it would be insane to blunder on through the dark, even if he had the strength. His need for rest was imperative and he thought: "I have played the fox, now I must play the cat of the fable."

A big tree with a thick trunk and outspread branches was nearby, and, taking care to leave not the slightest mark, he climbed up and, stretching out on one of the broad limbs, after a fashion, rested. Rest brought him new confidence and almost a feeling of security. Even so zealous a hunter as General Zaroff could not trace him here, he told himself; only the devil himself could follow that complicated trail through the jungle after dark. But, perhaps, the general was a devil. . . .

An apprehensive night crawled slowly by like a wounded snake, and sleep did not visit Rainsford, although the silence of a dead world was on the jungle. Toward morning when a dingy gray was varnishing the sky, the cry of some startled bird focused Rainsford's attention in that direction. Something was coming through the bush, coming slowly, carefully, coming by the same winding way Rainsford had come. He flattened himself down on the limb, and through a screen of leaves almost as thick as tapestry, he watched.

The thing that was approaching was a man.

It was General Zaroff. He made his way along with his eyes fixed in utmost concentration on the ground before him. He paused, almost beneath the tree, dropped to his knees and studied the ground. Rainsford's impulse was to hurl himself down like a panther, but he saw that the general's right hand held something metallic—a small automatic pistol.

The hunter shook his head several times, as if he were puzzled. Then he straightened up and took from his case one of his black cigarettes; its incenselike smoke floated up to Rainsford's nostrils.

Rainsford held his breath. The general's eyes had left the ground and were traveling inch by inch up the tree. Rainsford froze there, every muscle tensed for a spring. But the sharp eyes of the hunter stopped before they reached the limb where Rainsford lay; a smile spread over his brown face. Very deliberately he blew a smoke ring into the air; then he turned his back on the tree and walked carelessly away, back along the trail he had come. The swish of the underbrush against his hunting boots grew fainter and fainter.

The pent-up air burst hotly from Rainsford's lungs. His first thought made him feel sick and numb. The general could follow a trail through the woods at night; he could follow an extremely difficult trail; he must have uncanny powers; only by the merest chance had the Cossack failed to see his quarry.

Rainsford's second thought was even more terrible. It sent a shudder of cold horror through him. Why had the general smiled? Why had he turned back?

Rainsford did not want to believe what his reason told him was true, but the truth was as evident as the sun that by now had pushed through the morning mists. The general was playing with him! The general was saving him for another day's sport! The Cossack was the cat; he was the mouse. Then it was that Rainsford knew the full meaning of terror.

"I will not lose my nerve. I will not."

He slid down from the tree, and struck off again into the woods. His face was set and he forced the machinery of his mind to function. Three hundred yards from his hiding place he stopped where a huge dead tree leaned precariously on a smaller, living one. Throwing off his sack of food, Rainsford took his knife from its sheath and began to work with all his energy.

The job was finished at last, and he threw himself down behind a fallen log a hundred feet away. He did not have to wait long. The cat was coming again to play with the mouse.

Following the trail with the sureness of a bloodhound, came General Zaroff. Nothing escaped those searching black eyes, no crushed blade of grass, no bent twig, no mark, no matter how faint, in the moss. So intent was the Cossack on his stalking that he was upon the thing Rainsford had made before he saw it. His foot touched the protruding bough that was the trigger. Even as he touched it, the general sensed his danger and leaped back with the agility of an ape. But he was not quite quick enough; the dead tree, delicately adjusted to rest on the cut living one, crashed down and struck the general a glancing blow on the shoulder as it fell; but for his alertness, he must have been smashed beneath it. He staggered, but he did not fall; nor did he drop his revolver. He stood there, rubbing his injured shoulder; and Rainsford, with fear again gripping his heart, heard the general's mocking laugh ring through the jungle.

"Rainsford," called the general. "If you are

within the sound of my voice, as I suppose you are, let me congratulate you. Not many men know how to make a Malay man-catcher. Luckily for me, I, too, have hunted in Malacca. You are proving interesting, Mr. Rainsford. I am going now to have my wound dressed; it's only a slight one. But I shall be back. I shall be back."

When the general had gone, Rainsford took up his flight again. It was flight now, desperate, hopeless flight that carried him on for some hours. Dusk came, then darkness, and still he pressed on. The ground grew softer under his moccasins; the vegetation grew ranker, denser; insects bit him savagely. Then, as he stepped forward, his foot sank into the ooze. He tried to wrench it back, but the muck sucked viciously at his foot as if it were a giant leech. With a violent effort, he tore his foot loose. He knew where he was now. Death Swamp and its quicksand.

His hands were tight closed as if his nerve were something tangible that someone in the darkness was trying to tear from his grip. The softness of the earth had given him an idea. He stepped back from the quicksand a dozen feet or so and, like some huge prehistoric beaver, he began to dig.

Rainsford had dug himself in in France when a second's delay meant death. That had been a pleasant pastime compared to his digging now. The pit grew deeper; when it was above his shoulders, he climbed out and from some hard saplings cut stakes and sharpened them to a fine point. These stakes he planted in the bottom of the pit with the points sticking up. With flying fingers he wove a rough carpet of weeds and branches, and with it he covered the mouth of the pit. Then, wet with sweat and aching with tiredness, he crouched behind the stump of a lightning-charred tree.

He knew his pursuer was coming; he heard the padding sound of feet on the soft earth, and the night breeze brought him the perfume of the general's cigarette. It seemed to Rainsford that the general was coming with unusual swiftness; he was not feeling his way along, foot by foot. Rainsford, crouching there, could not see the general, nor could he see the pit. He lived a year in a minute. Then he felt an impulse to cry aloud with joy, for he heard the sharp scream of pain as the pointed stakes found their mark. He leaped up from his place of concealment. Then he cowered back. Three feet from the pit a man was standing, with an electric torch.

"You've done well, Rainsford," the voice of the general called. "Your Burmese tiger pit has claimed one of my best dogs. Again you score. I think, Mr. Rainsford, I'll see what you can do against my whole pack. I'm going home for a rest now. Thank you for a most amusing evening."

At daybreak Rainsford, lying near the swamp, was awakened by a sound that made him know that he had new things to learn about fear. It was a distant sound, faint and wavering; but he knew it. It was the baying of a pack of hounds.

Rainsford knew he could do one of two things.

He could stay where he was and wait. That was suicide. He could flee. That was postponing the inevitable. For a moment he stood there, thinking. An idea that held a wild chance came to him, and, tightening his belt, he headed away from the swamp. The baying of the hounds grew nearer. On a ridge Rainsford climbed a tree. Down a watercourse, not a quarter of a mile away, he could see the bush moving. Straining his eyes, he saw the lean figure of General Zaroff; just ahead of him Rainsford made out another figure whose wide shoulders surged through the tall jungle weeds; it was the giant Ivan, and he seemed pulled forward by some unseen force; Rainsford knew that Ivan must be holding the pack in leash.

They would be on him any minute now. His mind worked frantically. He thought of a native trick he had learned in Uganda. He slid down the tree. He caught hold of a springy young sapling and to it he fastened his hunting knife, with the blade pointing down the trail; with a bit of wild grapevine he tied back the sapling. Then he ran for his life. The hounds raised their voices as they hit the fresh scent. Rainsford knew now how an animal at bay feels.

He had to stop to get his breath. The baying of the hounds stopped abruptly; and Rainsford's heart stopped too. They must have reached the knife.

He shinned excitedly up a tree and looked back. His pursuers had stopped. But the hope that was in Rainsford's brain when he climbed died, for he saw in the shallow valley that General Zaroff was still on his feet. But Ivan was not. The knife, driven by the recoil of the springing tree, had not wholly failed.

Rainsford had hardly tumbled to the ground when the pack took up the cry again.

"Nerve, nerve, nerve!" he panted, as he dashed along. A blue gap showed between the trees dead ahead. Ever nearer drew the hounds. Rainsford forced himself on toward that gap. He reached it. It was the shore of the sea. Across a cove he could see the gloomy gray stone of the chateau. Twenty feet below him the sea rumbled and hissed. Rainsford hesitated. He heard the hounds. Then he leaped far out into the sea.

When the general and his pack reached the place by the sea, the Cossack stopped. For some minutes he stood regarding the blue-green expanse of water. He shrugged his shoulders. Then he sat down, took a drink of brandy from a silver flask, lit a perfumed cigarette, and hummed a bit from *Madame Butterfly*.

General Zaroff had an exceedingly good dinner in his great paneled dining hall that evening. With it he had a bottle of his rarest wine. Two slight annoyances kept him from perfect enjoyment. One was the thought that it would be difficult to replace Ivan; the other was that his quarry had escaped him; of course the American hadn't played the game—so thought the general as he tasted his after-dinner liqueur. In his library he read, to soothe himself, from the works of Marcus Aurelius. At ten he went up to his bedroom. He was deliciously tired, he said to himself, as he locked himself in. There was a little moonlight; so, before turning on his light, he went to the window and looked down at the courtyard. He could see the great hounds, and he called: "Better luck another time," to them. Then he switched on the light.

A man, who had been hiding in the curtains of the bed, was standing there.

"Rainsford!" screamed the general. "How did you get here?"

"Swam," said Rainsford. "I found it quicker than walking through the jungle."

The general sucked in his breath and smiled. "I congratulate you," he said. "You have won the game."

Rainsford did not smile. "I am still a beast at bay," he said, in a low, hoarse voice. "Get ready, General Zaroff." He reached quickly for two crossed swords hanging on the wall near him and tossed one over to the general.

The general made one of his deepest bows. "I see," he said. "Splendid! One of us is to furnish a repast for the hounds. The other will sleep in this very excellent bed. On guard, Rainsford."

He had never slept in a better bed, Rainsford decided.

CONTENTS OF THE DEAD MAN'S POCKET

JACK FINNEY

AT THE LITTLE LIVING-ROOM DESK Tom Benecke rolled two sheets of flimsy and a heavier top sheet, carbon paper sandwiched between them, into his portable. Interoffice Memo, the top sheet was headed, and he typed tomorrow's date just below this; then he glanced at a creased yellow sheet, covered with his own handwriting, beside the typewriter. "Hot in here," he muttered to himself. Then, from the short hallway at his back, he heard the muffled clang of wire coat hangers in the bedroom closet, and at this reminder of what his wife was doing he thought: Hot, hell—guilty conscience.

He got up, shoving his hands into the back pockets of his gray wash slacks, stepped to the living-room window beside the desk and stood breathing on the glass, watching the expanding circle of mist, staring down through the autumn night at Lexington Avenue, eleven stories below. He was a tall, lean, dark-haired young man in a pullover sweater, who looked as though he might have played basketball in college. Now he placed the heels of his hands against the top edge of the lower window frame and shoved upward. But as usual the window didn't budge, and he had to lower his hands and then shoot them hard upward to jolt the window open a few inches. He dusted his hands, muttering.

But still he didn't begin his work. He crossed the room to the hallway entrance and, leaning against the doorjamb, he called, "Clare?" When his wife answered, he said, "Sure you don't mind going alone?"

"No." Her voice was muffled, and he knew her head and shoulders were in the bedroom closet. Then the tap of her high heels sounded on the wood floor and she appeared at the end of the little hallway, both hands raised to one ear, clipping on an earring. She smiled at him—a slender, very pretty girl with light brown, almost blond hair—her prettiness emphasized by the pleasant nature that showed in her face. "It's just that I hate you to miss this movie; you wanted to see it too."

"Yeah, I know." He ran his fingers through his hair. "Got to get this done though."

She nodded, accepting this. Then, glancing at the desk across the living room, she said, "You work too much though, Tom—and too hard."

He smiled. "You won't mind though, will you, when the money comes rolling in and I'm known as the Boy Wizard of Wholesale Groceries?"

"I guess not." She smiled and turned back toward the bedroom.

At his desk again, Tom lit a cigarette and then a few moments later as Clare appeared, ready to leave, he set it on the rim of the ash tray. "Just after seven," she said. "I can make the beginning of the first feature."

He walked to the front-door closet to help her on with her coat. He kissed her then and, for an instant, holding her close, smelling the perfume she had used, he was tempted to go with her; it was not actually true that he had to work tonight, though he very much wanted to. This was his own project, unannounced as yet in his office, and it could be postponed. But then they won't see it till Monday, he thought once again, and if I give it to the boss tomorrow he might read it over the weekend. . . . "Have a good time," he said aloud. He opened the door for her, feeling the air from the building hallway, smelling faintly of floor wax, stream gently past his face.

He watched her walk down the hall, flicked a hand in response as she waved, and then he started to close the door, but it resisted for a moment. As the door opening narrowed, the current of warm air from the hallway, channeled through this smaller opening now, suddenly rushed past him with accelerated force. Behind him he heard the slap of the window curtains against the wall and the sound of paper fluttering from his desk, and he had to push to close the door.

Turning, he saw a sheet of white paper drifting to the floor in a series of arcs, and another sheet, yellow, moving toward the window, caught in the dying current flowing through the narrow opening. As he watched, the paper struck the bottom edge of the window and hung there for an instant, plastered against the glass and wood. Then as the moving air stilled completely the curtains swinging back from the wall to hang free again, he saw the yellow sheet drop to the window ledge and slide over out of sight.

He ran across the room, grasped the bottom edge of the window and tugged, staring through the glass. He saw the yellow sheet, dimly now in the darkness outside, lying on the ornamental ledge a yard below the window. Even as he watched, it was moving, scraping slowly along the ledge, pushed by the breeze that pressed steadily against the building wall. He heaved on the window with all his strength and it shot open with a bang, the window weight rattling in the casing. But the paper was past his reach and, leaning out into the night, he watched it scud steadily along the ledge to the south, half plastered against the building wall. Above the muffled sound of the street traffic far below, he could hear the dry scrape of its movement, like a leaf on the pavement.

The living room of the next apartment to the south projected a yard or more farther out toward the street than this one because the Beneckes paid seven and a half dollars less rent than their neighbors. And now the yellow sheet, sliding along the stone ledge, nearly invisible in the night, was stopped by the projecting blank wall of the next apartment. It lay motionless, then, in the corner formed by the two walls—a good five yards away, pressed firmly against the ornate corner ornament of the ledge, by the breeze that moved past Tom Benecke's face.

He knelt at the window and stared at the yellow paper for a full minute or more, waiting for it to move, to slide off the ledge and fall, hoping he could follow its course to the street, and then hurry down in the elevator and retrieve it. But it didn't move, and then he saw that the paper was caught firmly between a projection of the convoluted corner ornament and the ledge. He thought about the poker from the fireplace, then the broom, then the mop—discarding each thought as it occurred to him. There was nothing in the apartment long enough to reach that paper.

It was hard for him to understand that he actually had to abandon it—it was ridiculous—and he began to curse. Of all the papers on his desk, why did it have to be this one in particular! On four long Saturday afternoons he had stood in supermarkets counting the people who passed certain displays, and the results were scribbled on that yellow sheet. From stacks of trade publications, gone over page by page in snatched half hours at work and during evenings at home, he had copied facts, quotations, and figures onto that sheet. And he had carried it with him to the Public Library, where he'd spent a dozen lunch hours and early evenings adding more. All were needed to support and lend authority to his idea for a new grocery-store display method;

without them his idea was a mere opinion. And there they all lay, in his own improvised short-hand—countless hours of work—out there on the ledge.

For many seconds he believed he was going to abandon the yellow sheet, that there was nothing to do. The work could be duplicated. But it would take two months, and the time to present this idea, damn it, was now, for use in the spring displays. He struck his fist on the window ledge. Then he shrugged. Even though his plan were adopted, he told himself, it wouldn't bring him a raise in pay—not immediately, anyway, or as a direct result. It won't bring me a promotion either, he argued—not of itself.

But just the same, and he couldn't escape the thought, this and other independent projects, some already done and others planned for the future, would gradually mark him out from the score of other young men in his company. They were the way to change from a name on the pay-roll to a name in the minds of the company officials. They were the beginning of the long, long climb to where he was determined to be, at the very top. And he knew he was going out there in the darkness, after the yellow sheet.

By a kind of instinct, he instantly began making his intention acceptable to himself by laughing at it. The mental picture of himself sidling along the ledge outside was absurd—it was actually comical—and he smiled. He imagined himself describing it; it would make a good story at the office and, it occurred to him, would add a special interest and importance to his memorandum, which would do it no harm.

To simply go out and get his paper was an easy task—he could be back here with it in less than two minutes—and he knew he wasn't deceiving himself. The ledge, he saw, measuring it with his eye, was about as wide as the length of his shoe, and perfectly flat. And every fifth row of brick in the face of the building, he remembered—leaning out, he verified this—was indented half an inch, enough for the tips of his fingers, enough to maintain balance easily. It occurred to him that if this ledge and wall were only a yard above ground—as he knelt at the window staring out, this thought was the final confirmation of his intention—he could move along the ledge indefinitely.

On a sudden impulse, he got to his feet, walked to the front closet and took out an old tweed jacket; it would be cold outside. He put it on and buttoned it as he crossed the room rapidly toward the open window. In the back of his mind he knew he'd better hurry before he thought too much, and at the window he didn't allow himself to hesitate.

He swung a leg over the sill, then felt for the ledge a yard below the window with his foot. Gripping the bottom of the window frame very tightly and carefully, he slowly ducked his head under it, feeling on his face the sudden change from the warm air of the room to the chill outside. With infinite care he brought out his other leg, his mind concentrating on what he was do-

ing. Then he slowly stood erect. Most of the
putty, dried out and brittle, had dropped off the
bottom edging of the window frame, and the
flat wooden edging provided a good gripping
surface, a half inch or more deep, for the tips
of his fingers.

Now, balanced easily and firmly, he stood on
the edge outside in the slight, chill breeze, eleven
stories above the street, staring into his own
lighted apartment, odd and different-seeming
now.

First his right hand, then his left, he carefully
shifted his fingertip grip from the puttyless window ledging to an indented row of bricks directly to his right. It was hard to take the first
shuffling sideways step then—to make himself
move—and the fear stirred in his stomach, but
he did it, again by not allowing himself time to
think. And now—with his chest, stomach, and the
left side of his face pressed against the rough
cold brick—his lighted apartment was suddenly
gone, and it was much darker out here than he
had thought.

Without pause he continued—right foot, left
foot, right foot, left—his shoes shuffling and
scraping along the rough stone, never lifting
from it, fingers sliding along the exposed edging of bricks. He moved on the balls of his feet,
heels lifted slightly; the ledge was not quite as
wide as he'd expected. But leaning slightly in-
ward toward the face of the building and pressed
firmly against it, he could feel his balance firm
and secure, and moving along the ledge was quite
as easy as he had thought it would be. He could

hear the buttons of his jacket scraping steadily along the rough bricks and feel them catch momentarily, tugging a little, at each mortared crack. He simply did not permit himself to look down, though the compulsion to do so never left him; nor did he allow himself actually to think. Mechanically—right foot, left foot, over and again—he shuffled along crabwise, watching the projecting wall ahead loom steadily closer. . . .

Then he reached it and, at the corner—he'd decided how he was going to pick up the paper—he lifted his right foot and placed it carefully on the ledge that ran along the projecting wall at a right angle to the ledge on which his other foot rested. And now, facing the building, he stood in the corner formed by the two walls, one foot on the ledging of each, a hand on the shoulder-high indentation of each wall. His forehead was pressed directly into the corner against the cold bricks, and now he carefully lowered first one hand, then the other, perhaps a foot farther down, to the next indentation in the rows of bricks.

Very slowly, sliding his forehead down the trough of the brick corner and bending his knees, he lowered his body toward the paper lying between his outstretched feet. Again he lowered his fingerholds another foot and bent his knees still more, thigh muscles taut, his forehead sliding and bumping down the brick V. Half squatting, he dropped his left hand to the next indentation and then slowly reached with his right hand toward the paper.

He couldn't quite touch it, and his knees now

were pressed against the wall; he could bend them no farther. But by ducking his head another inch lower, the top of his head now pressed against the bricks, he lowered his right shoulder and his fingers had the paper by a corner, pulling it loose. At the same instant he saw, between his legs and far below, Lexington Avenue stretched out for miles ahead.

He saw, in that instant, the Loew's theatre sign, blocks ahead; the miles of traffic signals; the lights of cars and street lamps; countless neon signs; and the moving dots of people. And a violent, instantaneous explosion of absolute terror roared through him. For an instant he saw himself externally—bent practically double, balanced on this narrow ledge, nearly half his body projecting out above the street far below—and he began to tremble violently, panic flaring through mind and muscles.

In the fractional moment before horror paralyzed him, as he stared between his legs at that length of street far beneath him, a fragment of his mind raised his body in a spasmodic jerk to an upright position again, but so violently that his head scraped hard against the wall, bouncing off it, and his body swayed outward to the knife edge of balance, and he very nearly plunged backward and fell. Then he was leaning far into the corner again, pushing into it, not only his face but his chest and stomach, his back arching; and his finger tips clung with all the pressure of his pulling arms to the shoulder-high half-inch indentation in the bricks.

He was more than trembling now; his whole

body was racked with violent shuddering beyond control, his eyes squeezed so tightly shut it was painful, though he was past awareness of that. His teeth were exposed in a frozen grimace, the strength draining like water from his knees. It was extremely likely that he would faint, to slump down along the wall, and then drop backward, a limp weight, out into nothing. And to save his life he concentrated on holding onto consciousness, drawing deep breaths of cold air into his lungs, fighting to keep his senses aware.

Then he knew he would not faint, but he could not stop shaking nor open his eyes. He stood where he was, breathing deeply, trying to hold back the terror of the glimpse of what lay below him; and he knew he had made a mistake in not making himself stare down at the street, getting used to it and accepting it, when he had first stepped out.

It was impossible to walk back. He couldn't bring himself to make the slightest movement. The strength was gone from his legs; his shivering hands—numb, cold and desperately rigid—had lost all deftness; his ability to move and balance was gone. Within a step or two, if he tried to move, he knew he would stumble clumsily and fall.

Seconds passed, with the chill faint wind pressing the side of his face, and he could hear the toned-down volume of the street traffic far beneath him. Again and again it slowed and then stopped, almost to silence; then presently, even this high, he would hear the click of the traffic signals and the subdued roar of the cars. During a lull in the sounds, he called out. Then he was shouting *"Help!"* so loudly it rasped his throat. But the pressure of the wind, moving between his face and the blank wall, snatched up his cries as he uttered them, and he knew they must sound directionless and distant. And he remembered how habitually, here in New York, he himself heard and ignored shouts in the night. If anyone heard him, there was no sign of it, and presently Tom Benecke knew he had to try moving; there was nothing else he could do.

Eyes squeezed shut, he watched scenes in his mind like scraps of motion-picture film. He saw himself stumbling suddenly sideways as he crept along the ledge and saw his body arc outward, arms flailing. He saw himself falling with terrible speed as his body revolved in the air, knees clutched tight to his chest, eyes squeezed shut, moaning softly.

Out of utter necessity, knowing that any of these thoughts might be a reality in the very next seconds, he was slowly able to shut his mind against every thought but what he now began to do. With fear-soaked slowness, he slid his left foot an inch or two toward his own impossibly distant window. Then he slid the fingers of his shivering left hand a corresponding distance. For a moment he could not bring himself to lift his right foot from one ledge to the other; then he did it, and became aware of the harsh exhalation of air from his throat and realized that he was panting. As his right hand, then, began to slide along the brick edging, he was astonished to feel the yellow paper pressed to the bricks underneath his stiff fingers, and he uttered a terrible, abrupt bark that might have been a laugh or a moan. He opened his mouth and took the paper in his teeth, pulling it out from under his fingers.

By a kind of trick—by concentrating his entire mind on first his left foot, then his left hand, then the other foot, then the other hand—he was able to move, almost imperceptibly, trembling steadily, very nearly without thought. But he could feel the terrible strength of that pent-up horror on just the other side of the flimsy barrier he had erected in his mind; and he knew that if it broke through he would lose this thin artificial control of his body.

During one slow step he tried keeping his eyes closed; it made him feel safer, shutting him off a little from the fearful reality of where he was. Then a sudden rush of giddiness swept over him and he had to open his eyes wide, staring sideways at the cold rough brick and angled lines of mortar, his cheek tight against the building. He kept his eyes open then, knowing that if he once let them flick outward, to stare for an instant at the lighted windows across the street, he would be past help.

He didn't know how many dozens of tiny sidling steps he had taken, his chest, belly and face pressed to the wall; but he knew the slender hold he was keeping on his mind and body was going to break. He had a sudden mental picture of his apartment on just the other side of this wall—warm, incredibly spacious. And he saw himself striding through it, lying down on the floor, arms spread wide, reveling in its unbelievable security. The remoteness of this utter safety, the contrast between it and where he now stood, was more than he could bear. And the barrier broke then, and the fear coursed through his nerves and muscles.

A fraction of his mind knew he was going to fall, and he began taking rapid blind steps with no feeling of what he was doing, sidling with a clumsy desperate swiftness, fingers scrabbling along the brick, almost hopelessly to the sudden backward pull and swift motion outward and down. Then his moving left hand slid onto not brick but sheer emptiness, an impossible gap in the face of the wall.

His right foot smashed into his left ankle bone; he staggered sideways, began falling, and the claw of his hand cracked against glass and wood, slid down it, and his finger tips were pressed hard on the puttyless edging of his window. His right hand smacked gropingly beside it as he fell to his knees; and, under the full weight and direct downward pull of his sagging body, the open window dropped shudderingly in its frame till it closed and his wrists struck the sill and were jarred off.

For a single moment he knelt, knee bones against stone on the very edge of the ledge, body swaying and touching nowhere else, fighting for balance. Then he lost it, his shoulders plunging backward, and he flung his arms forward, his hands smashing against the window casing on either side; and—his body moving backward—his fingers clutched the narrow wood stripping of the upper pane.

For an instant he hung suspended between balance and falling, his fingertips hooked to these slim edgings of wood. Elbows slowly bending, he began to draw the full weight of his upper body forward, knowing that the instant his fingers slipped off these quarter-inch strips he'd plunge backward and be falling. Elbows imperceptibly bending, body shaking with the strain, the sweat starting from his forehead in great sudden drops, he pulled, his entire thought concentrated in his finger tips. Then suddenly, the strain slackened, his chest touching the window sill, and he was kneeling on the ledge, his forehead pressed to the closed window.

Dropping his palms to the sill; he stared into his living room—at the brown davenport, and a magazine he had left there; at the pictures on the walls and the gray rug; at his papers, typewriter and desk, not two feet from his nose. A movement from his desk caught his eye and he saw a thin curl of blue smoke; his cigarette, the ash long, was still burning in the ash tray where he'd left it—this was past all belief—only a few minutes before.

His head moved, and in faint reflection from the glass before him he saw the yellow paper clenched in his teeth. Lifting a hand from the sill he took it from his mouth; the moistened corner parted, and he spat it out.

For a moment, in the light from the living

room, he stared wonderingly at the yellow sheet in his hand and then crushed it into the side pocket of his jacket.

He couldn't open the window. It had been pulled down and completely closed, but its lower edge was below the level of the outside sill; there was no room to get his fingers underneath it. Between the upper sash and the lower was a gap not wide enough to get his fingers into; he couldn't push it open. The upper window panel, he knew from long experience, was frozen tight with dried paint.

Very carefully observing his balance, the finger tips of his left hand again hooked to the narrow stripping of the window casing, he drew back his right hand, palm facing the glass, and then struck the glass with the heel of his hand.

His arm rebounded from the pane, his body tottering, and he knew he didn't dare strike a harder blow.

But in the security and relief of his new position, he simply smiled; with only a sheet of glass between him and the room just before him, it was not possible that there wasn't a way past it. Eyes narrowing, he thought for a few moments. But nothing occurred to him. Still, he felt calm: the trembling, he realized, had stopped. At the back of his mind there still lay the thought that once he was again in his home, he could give release to his feelings. He actually *would* lie on the floor, rolling, clenching tufts of the rug in his hands. He would literally run across the room, free to move as he liked, testing and reveling in his absolute security, letting the relief flood through him, draining the fear from his mind and body. His yearning for this was astonishingly intense, and somehow he knew he had better keep this feeling at bay.

He took a half dollar from his pocket and struck it against the pane, but without any hope that the glass would break and with very little disappointment when it did not. After a few moments he drew his leg up onto the ledge and picked loose his shoelace. He slipped off the shoe and, holding it across the instep, drew back his arm as far as he dared and struck the leather heel against the glass. The pane rattled, but he knew he'd been a long way from breaking it. His foot was cold and he slipped the shoe back on. He shouted again, experimentally, but there was no answer.

The realization suddenly struck him that he might have to wait here till Clare came home, and for a moment the thought was funny. He could see Clare opening the front door, withdrawing her key from the lock, closing the door behind her and then glancing up to see him crouched on the other side of the window. He could see her rush across the room, face astounded and frightened, and hear himself shouting instructions: "Never mind how I got here! Just open the wind—" She couldn't open it, he remembered; she'd always had to call him. She'd have to get the building superintendent or a neighbor, and he pictured himself smiling and answering their questions as he climbed in. "I just wanted to get a breath of fresh air, so—"

He couldn't possibly wait here till Clare came home. It was the second feature she'd wanted to see, and she'd left in time to see the first. She'd be three hours or— He glanced at his watch. Clare had been gone eight minutes. Only eight minutes ago he had kissed his wife good-bye.

It would be four hours before she could possibly be home, and he tried to picture himself kneeling out here, finger tips hooked to these narrow strippings, while first one movie began, developed, reached its climax, and then finally ended. There'd be a newsreel next, maybe, and then a cartoon, and then interminable scenes from coming pictures. And then, once more, the beginning of a full-length picture—while all the time he hung out here. . . .

He might possibly get to his feet, but he was afraid to try. Already his legs were cramped, his thigh muscles tired; his knees hurt, his feet felt numb and his hands were stiff. He couldn't possibly stay out here for four hours, or anywhere near it. Long before that his legs and arms would give out; he would be forced to try changing his position often—stiffly, clumsily, his coordination and strength gone—and he would fall. Quite realistically, he knew no one could stay on this ledge for four hours.

A dozen windows in the apartment building across the street were lighted. Looking over his shoulder, he could see the top of a man's head behind a newspaper. In another window he saw the blue-gray flicker of a television screen. No more than twenty-odd yards from his back were scores of people, and if just one of them would walk idly to his window and glance out. . . . For some moments he stared over his shoulder at the lighted rectangles, waiting. But no one appeared. The man reading his paper turned a page. A figure passed another of the windows and was immediately gone.

In the inside pocket of his jacket he found a little sheaf of papers, and he pulled one out and looked at it in the light from the living room. It was an old letter, an advertisement of some sort; his name and address, in purple ink, were on a label pasted to the envelope. Gripping one end of the envelope in his teeth, he twisted it into a tight curl. From his shirt pocket he took a book of matches. He didn't dare let go the casing with both hands but, with the twist of paper in his teeth, he opened the matchbook with his free hand; then he bent one of the matches in two without tearing it from the folder, its red-tipped end now touching the striking surface. With his thumb, he rubbed the red tip across the striking end.

He did it again, then again, and still again, pressing harder each time, and the match suddenly flared, burning his thumb. But he kept it alight, shielding it with his body. He held the flame to the paper in his mouth till it caught. Then he snuffed out the match with his thumb and forefinger, careless of the burn, and replaced the book in his pocket. Taking the paper in his hand, he held it flame down, watching the flame crawl up the paper, till it flared bright. Then he held it behind him over the street, moving it from side to side, the flame flickering and guttering in the wind.

There were three more letters in his pocket

and he lit each of them, holding each till the flame touched his hand and then dropping it to the street below. At one point, watching over his shoulder while the last of the letters burned, he saw the man across the street put down his paper and stand—even seeming, to Tom, to glance toward his window. But when he moved, it was only to walk across the room.

There were a dozen coins in Tom Benecke's pocket and he dropped them, three or four at a time. But if they struck anyone, or if anyone noticed their falling, no one connected them with their source.

His arms had begun to tremble from the steady strain of clinging to this narrow perch, and he did not know what to do now and was terribly frightened. Clinging to the window stripping with one hand, he again searched his pockets. But now—he had left his wallet on his dresser when he'd changed clothes—there was nothing but the yellow sheet. It occurred to him irrelevantly that his death on the sidewalk would be an eternal mystery; the window closed—why, how, and from where could he have fallen? No one would be able to identify his body for a time, either—the thought was somehow unbearable and increased his fear. All they'd find in his pockets would be the yellow sheet. Contents of the dead man's pockets, one sheet of paper bearing penciled notations—incomprehensible.

He understood fully that he might actually be going to die; his arms, maintaining his balance, were trembling steadily now. And it occurred to him then with all the force of revelation that, if he fell, all he was ever going to have out of life he would then, abruptly, have had. Nothing, then, could ever be changed; and nothing more —no least experience or pleasure—could ever be added to his life. He wished, then, that he had not allowed his wife to go off by herself tonight —and on similar nights. He thought of all the evenings he had spent away from her, working; and he regretted them. He thought wonderingly of his fierce ambition and of the direction his life had taken; he thought of the hours he'd spent by himself, filling the yellow sheet that had brought him out here. Contents of the dead man's pockets, he thought with sudden fierce anger, a wasted life.

He was simply not going to cling here till he slipped and fell; he told himself that now. There was one last thing he could try; he had been aware of it for some moments, refusing to think about it, but now he faced it. Kneeling here on the ledge, the fingertips of one hand pressed to the narrow strip of wood, he could draw his other hand back a yard perhaps, fist clenched tight, very slowly till he sensed the outer limit of balance, then, as hard as he was able, he could drive his fist forward against the glass. If it broke, his fist smashing through, he was safe; he might cut himself badly, and probably would, but with his arm inside the room, he could be secure. But if the glass did not break, the rebound, flinging his arm back, would topple him off the ledge.

He tested his plan. The fingers of his left hand clawlike on the little stripping, he drew back his other fist until his body began teetering backward. But he had no leverage now—he could feel there would be no force to his swing—and he moved his fist slowly forward on his knees again and could sense his swing would carry its greatest force. Glancing down, measuring the distance from his fist to the glass, he saw it was less than two feet.

It occurred to him he could raise his arm over his head, to bring it down against the glass. But, experimenting in slow motion, he knew it would be an awkward girl-like blow without the force of a driving punch, and not nearly enough to break the glass.

Facing the window, he had to drive a blow from the shoulder at a distance of less than two feet; and he did not know whether it would break through the heavy glass. It might; he could picture it happening, he could feel it in the nerves of his arm. And it might not; he could feel that too—feel his fist striking this glass and being instantaneously flung back by the unbreaking pane, feel the fingers of his other hand breaking loose.

He waited, arm drawn back, fist balled, but in no hurry to strike; this pause, he knew, might be an extension of his life. And to live even a few seconds longer, he felt, even out here on this ledge in the night, was infinitely better than to die a moment earlier than he had to. His arm grew tired, and he brought it down and rested it.

Then he knew it was time to make the attempt. He could not kneel here hesitating indefinitely till he lost all courage to act, waiting till he slipped off the ledge. Again he drew back his arm, knowing this time that he would not bring it down till he struck. His elbow protruding over Lexington Avenue far below, the fingers of his other hand pressed down bloodlessly tight against the narrow stripping, he waited, feeling the sick tenseness and terrible excitement building. It grew and swelled toward the moment of action, his nerves tautening. He thought of Clare —just a wordless, yearning thought—and then drew his arm back just a bit more, fist so tight his fingers pained him, and knowing he was going to do it. Then with full power, with every last scrap of strength he could bring to bear, he shot his arm forward toward the glass, and he said "Clare!"

He heard the sound, felt the blow, felt himself falling forward, and his hand closed on the living room curtains, the shards and fragments of glass showering onto the floor. And then, kneeling there on the ledge, an arm thrust into the room up to the shoulder, he began picking away the protruding slivers and great wedges of glass from the window frame, tossing them in onto the rug. And, as he grasped the edges of the empty window frame and climbed into his home, he was grinning in triumph.

He did not lie down on the floor or run through the apartment, as he had promised himself; even in the first few moments it seemed to him natural and normal that he should be where he was. He simply turned to his desk, pulled the crumpled yellow sheet from his pocket and laid it down where it had been, smoothing it out; then he absently laid a pencil across it to weight it down. He shook his head wonderingly, and turned to walk toward the closet.

There he got out his topcoat and hat and, without waiting to put them on, opened the front door and stepped out, to go find his wife. He turned to pull the door closed and the warm air from the hall rushed through the narrow opening again. As he saw the yellow paper, the pencil flying, scooped off the desk and, unimpeded by the glassless window, sail out into the night and out of his life, Tom Benecke burst into laughter and then closed the door.

AS BEST HE CAN
GEOFFREY HOUSEHOLD

"WE ARE SAFE HERE, DOMINIQUE?"

"Quite safe, mon commandant. The Boches never move outside their camp at night. And there is nothing to do in these sand dunes."

"But you take a risk with that light."

"It cannot be seen. We are down in a hollow, and my pickets are out all round us."

"And no Boches on the beach?"

"They are forbidden to walk on the beach after dark. It might not be healthy."

"But the relations of your district with the camp are correct?"

"Quite correct, mon commandant. If anything happens, we are careful it should appear an accident. The Boches have forgotten we are Frenchmen."

"They find too many collaborators."

"Some. It's inevitable. But all are harmless, except this prisoner with whom I wish the court to deal. He could betray us if he wished."

"It is a question of the death sentence?"

"That is for the court to decide. Hitherto Dumetrier has refused any explanation of his behavior."

"I see. Well, Dominique, my colleagues and I are ready if you will bring him before us. . . . Oh, but he's a fine looking type! . . . One would be sure of getting a decent bottle at his establishment. . . . Your name?"

"Louis Alphonse Dumetrier. And yours?"

"You may address me as the President of the Court."

"Very well, M. le Président."

"Your occupation?"

"Café proprietor."

"Have you any objection to the court?"

"Not the slightest M. le Président—except that it is held in the middle of the night when a businessman like myself should be asleep."

"You can be put to sleep for a very long time!"

"In that case may I request that they do not make a mess of it as they did when poor Charles Yonne had an accident with his gun in passing through a hedge?"

"You are well informed, Dumetrier."

"A café proprietor overhears much, M. le Président."

"Therefore his loyalty must be beyond question."

"Do you think then that we of the Resistance have not wives and children?"

"There is no need for excitement. Each of us serves as best he can."

"Dumetrier, it is not service to rescue German soldiers from the sea. M. Dominique, whose position in the Resistance you unfortunately know, demands an investigation of your motives."

"I doubt if M. Dominique has closely regarded the circumstances, M. le Président."

"Very well. We know the difficulties of Frenchmen, and you will not find the court unsympathetic. Tell us a little of your life."

"What is there to tell? In the summer, before the war, I made what I could from holiday visitors; for the rest of the year, there were the regular clients—a few farmers, a few fishermen. And on fine Sundays in spring and autumn there would be parties for lunch."

"And now?"

"Well, M. le Président, as M. Dominique will have told you, I am on excellent terms with the Boches. And as I usually have a few delicacies from their army rations, it makes life easier for us all."

"That is because you make a habit of trying to save them from drowning?"

"Hardly a habit, M. le Président. There were only three. And a little effort impresses the Boches."

"Before the war you were commended for gallantry in saving life, I believe?"

"There was no damned gallantry! It's all a farce for a man who knows the beaches as I do. Look, M. le Président, our beach is safe for children who never venture beyond the breakers and safe for a strong swimmer who is not afraid of the current. But for young people who have been trained in swimming pools and think they know it all—there is the danger!"

"There have been fatalities?"

"Fewer than you would think. One is always on the watch. I am no Channel swimmer, M. le Président, but I know the breakers and, without exaggeration, I can do in the water what I wish."

"So the court understands. But what is incredible, Dumetrier, is that you treat the enemy like young Frenchmen on holiday. Do not shrug your shoulders! France is occupied! It is no time for humanity!"

"Humanity does not interest me, M'sieur."

"What then? What then? Do you deny that on three separate occasions you have risked your life to rescue German soldiers? You do not think of your wife and children then, scum of a collaborator!"

"No. When it is a question of Germans, I do not think of my wife and children."

"But it is unbelievable! This animal prefers to his family some damned Boches who are in difficulties and have not the strength to get back to shore!"

"I do not know whether they had the strength or not, M. le Président. When strong swimmers are waiting for a wave to bring them in, it is very hard to see from the beach if they are really in trouble."

"But you were ready to assume they were!"

"Oh, yes, I always assumed they were."

"And was it necessary to save them?"

"I do not think it was always necessary."

"And yet you admit risking your life to bring them in!"

"M. le Président, I admit I brought them in. But they were none of them alive when we reached shore. . . ."

TOO EARLY SPRING
STEPHEN VINCENT BENET

I'M WRITING THIS DOWN because I don't ever
want to forget the way it was. It doesn't seem
as if I could, now, but they all tell you things
change. And I guess they're right. Older people
must have forgotten or they couldn't be the
way they are. And that goes for even the best
ones, like Dad and Mr. Grant. They try to understand, but they don't seem to know how. And
the others make you feel dirty, or else they make
you feel like a goof. Till, pretty soon, you begin
to forget yourself—you begin to think, "Well,
maybe they're right and it was that way." And
that's the end of everything. So I've got to write
this down. Because they smashed it forever—
but it wasn't the way they said.

Mr. Grant always says in comp. class: "Begin

at the beginning." Only I don't know quite where the beginning was. We had a good summer at Big Lake but it was just the same summer. I worked pretty hard at the practice basket I rigged up in the barn, and I learned how to do the back jackknife. I'll never dive like Kerry, but you want to be as all-around as you can. And when I took my measurements, at the end of the summer, I was 5 ft. 9¾ and I'd gained 12 lbs. 6 ozs. That isn't bad for going on sixteen, and the old chest expansion was O.K. You don't want to get too heavy, because basketball's a fast game, but the year before was the year when I got my height, and I was so skinny, I got tired. But this year, Kerry helped me practice a couple of times, and he seemed to think I had a good chance for the team. So I felt pretty set up—they'd never had a sophomore on it before. And Kerry's a natural athlete, so that means a lot from him. He's a pretty good brother too. Most juniors at State wouldn't bother with a fellow in high school.

It sounds as if I were trying to run away from what I have to write down, but I'm not. I want to remember the summer, too, because it's the last happy one I'll ever have. Oh, when I'm an old man—thirty or forty—things may be all right again. But that's a long time to wait and it won't be the same.

And yet, that summer was different, too, in a way. So it must have started then, though I didn't know it. I went around with the gang as usual and we had a good time. But, every now

and then, it would strike me we were acting
like awful kids. They thought I was getting a
big head, but I wasn't. It just wasn't much fun
—even going to the cave. It was like still playing
marbles when you're in high school.

I had sense enough not to try to tag after
Kerry and his crowd. You can't do that. But when
they all got out on the lake in canoes, warm
evenings, and somebody brought a phonograph
along, I used to go down to the Point, all by
myself, and listen and listen. Maybe they'd be
talking or maybe they'd be singing, but it all
sounded mysterious across the water. I wasn't
trying to hear what they said, you know. That's
the kind of thing Tot Pickens does. I'd just listen
with my arms around my knees—and somehow
it would hurt me to listen—and yet I'd rather do
that than be with the gang.

I was sitting under the four pines one night
right down by the edge of the water. There was
a big moon and they were singing. It's funny
how you can be unhappy and nobody knows it
but yourself.

I was thinking about Sheila Coe. She's Kerry's
girl. They fight but they get along. She's awfully
pretty and she can swim like a fool. Once Kerry
sent me over with her tennis racket and we had
quite a conversation. She was fine. And she didn't
pull any of this big-sister stuff, either, the way
some girls will with a fellow's kid brother.

And when the canoe came along, by the edge
of the lake, I thought for a moment it was her.
I thought maybe she was looking for Kerry and

maybe she'd stop and maybe she'd feel like talking to me again. I don't know why I thought that—I didn't have any reason. Then I saw it was just the Sharon kid, with a new kind of hairdo that made her look grown-up, and I felt sore. She didn't have any business out on the lake at her age. She was just a sophomore in high school, the same as me.

I chucked a stone in the water and it splashed right by the canoe, but she didn't squeal. She just said, "Fish," and chuckled. It struck me it was a kid's trick, trying to scare a kid.

"Hello, Helen," I said. "Where'd you swipe the gunboat?"

"They don't know I've got it," she said. "Oh, hello, Chuck Peters. How's Big Lake?"

"All right," I said. "How was camp?"

"It was peachy," she said. "We had a peachy counselor, Miss Morgan. She was on the Wellesley field-hockey team."

"Well," I said, "we missed your society." Of course we hadn't because they're across the lake and don't swim at our raft. But you ought to be polite.

"Thanks," she said. "Did you do the special reading for English? I thought it was dumb."

"It's always dumb," I said. "What canoe is that?"

"It's the old one," she said. "I'm not supposed to have it out at night. But you won't tell anybody, will you?"

"Be your age," I said. I felt generous. "I'll paddle a while, if you want," I said.

"All right," she said, so she brought it in and I got aboard. She went back in the bow and I took the paddle. I'm not strong on carting kids around, as a rule. But it was better than sitting there by myself.

"Where do you want to go?" I said.

"Oh, back toward the house," she said in a shy kind of voice. "I ought to really. I just wanted to hear the singing."

I didn't paddle fast, just let her slip. There was a lot of moon on the water. We kept around the edge so they wouldn't notice us. The singing sounded as if it came from a different country, a long way off.

She was a sensible kid, she didn't ask fool questions or giggle about nothing at all. Even when we went by Petters' Cove. That's where the lads from the bungalow colony go and it's pretty well populated on a warm night. You can hear them talking in low voices and now and then a laugh. Once Tot Pickens and a gang went over there with a flashlight, and a big guy chased them half a mile.

I felt funny, going there with her. But I said, "Well, it's certainly Old Home Week"—in an offhand tone, because, after all, you've got to be sophisticated. And she said, "People are funny," in just the right sort of way. I took quite a shine to her after that and we talked. The Sharons had only been in town three years and somehow I'd never really noticed her before. Mrs. Sharon's awfully good-looking, but she and Mr. Sharon fight. That's hard on a kid. And she was a quiet kid. She had a small kind of face and her eyes were sort of like a kitten's. You could see she got a great kick out of pretending to be grown-up—and yet it wasn't all pretending. A couple of times, I felt just as if I were talking to Sheila Coe. Only more comfortable, because, after all, we were the same age.

Do you know, after we put the canoe up, I walked all the way back home, around the lake? And most of the way, I ran. I felt swell too. I felt as if I could run forever and not stop. It was like finding something. I hadn't imagined anybody could feel the way I did about some things. And here was another person, even if it was a girl.

Kerry's door was open when I went by and he stuck his head out, and grinned.

"Well, kid," he said. "Stepping out?"

"Sure. With Greta Garbo," I said, and grinned back to show I didn't mean it. I felt sort of light-headed, with the run and everything.

"Look here, kid—" he said, as if he was going to say something. Then he stopped. But there was a funny look on his face.

And yet I didn't see her again till we were both back in High. Mr. Sharon's uncle died, back East, and they closed the cottage suddenly. But all the rest of the time at Big Lake I kept remembering that night and her little face. If I'd seen her in daylight, first, it might have been different. No, it wouldn't have been.

All the same, I wasn't even thinking of her when we bumped into each other the first day of school. It was raining and she had on a green slicker and her hair was curly under her hat. We grinned and said hello and had to run. But something happened to us, I guess.

I'll say this now—it wasn't like Tot Pickens and Mabel Palmer. It wasn't like Junior David and Betty Page—though they've been going together ever since kindergarten. It wasn't like any of those things. We didn't get sticky and sloppy. It wasn't like going with a girl.

There'd be days and days when we'd hardly see each other except in class. I had basketball practice almost every afternoon and she was taking music lessons four times a week. But you don't have to be always twos-ing with a person, if you feel that way about them. You seem to know the way they're thinking and feeling, the way you know yourself.

Now let me describe her. She had that little face and the eyes like a kitten's. When it rained, her hair curled all over the back of her neck. Her hair was yellow. She wasn't a tall girl but she wasn't clunky—just light and well-made and quick. She was awfully alive without being nervous—she never bit her fingernails or chewed the end of her pencil, but she'd answer quicker than anyone in the class. Nearly everybody liked her, but she wasn't best friends with any particular girl, the mushy way they get. The teachers all thought a lot of her, even Miss Eagles. Well, I had to spoil that.

If we'd been like Tot and Mabel we could have had a lot more time together, I guess. But

Helen isn't a liar and I'm not a snake. It wasn't easy, going over to her house, because Mr. and Mrs. Sharon would be polite to each other in front of you, and yet there'd be something wrong. And she'd have to be fair to both of them and they were always pulling at her. But we'd look at each other across the table and then it would be all right.

I don't know when it was that we knew we'd get married to each other sometime. We just started talking about it one day as if we always had. We were sensible, we knew it couldn't happen right off. We thought maybe when we were eighteen. That was two years, but we knew we had to be educated. You don't get as good a job if you aren't. Or that's what people say.

We weren't mushy either like some people. We got to kissing each other good-bye sometimes, because that's what you do when you're in love. It was cool, the way she kissed you; it was like leaves. But lots of times we wouldn't even talk about getting married, we'd just play checkers or go over the old Latin, or once in a while go to the movies with the gang. It was really a wonderful winter. I played every game after the first one, and she'd sit in the stands and watch, and I'd know she was there. You could see her little green hat or her yellow hair. Those are the school colors, green and gold.

And it's a queer thing, but everybody seemed to be pleased. That's what I can't get over. They liked to see us together. The grown people, I mean. Oh, of course, we got kidded too. And old Mrs. Withers would ask me about "my little sweetheart," in that awful damp voice of hers. But mostly, they were all right. Even Mother was all right, though she didn't like Mrs. Sharon. I did hear her say to Father, once, "Really, George how long is this going to last? Sometimes I feel as if I just couldn't stand it."

Then Father chuckled and said to her, "Now, Mary, last year you were worried about him because he didn't take any interest in girls at all."

"Well," she said, "he still doesn't. Oh, Helen's a nice child—no credit to Eva Sharon—and, thank heaven, she doesn't giggle. Well, Charles is mature for his age too. But he acts so solemn with her. It isn't natural."

"Oh, let Charlie alone," said Father. "The boy's all right. He's just got a one-track mind."

But it wasn't so nice for us after the spring came. In our part of the state, it comes pretty late, as a rule. But it was early this year. The little kids were out with scooters when usually they'd still be having snowfights and all of a sudden the radiators in the classrooms smelt dry. You'd got used to that smell for months—and then there was a day when you hated it again and everybody kept asking to open the windows. The monitors had a tough time, that first week—they always do when spring starts—but this year it was worse than ever because it came when you didn't expect it.

Usually, basketball's over by the time spring really breaks, but this year, it hit us while we still had three games to play. And it certainly played hell with us as a team. After Bladesburg nearly licked us, Mr. Grant called off part of practice till the day before the St. Matthew's game. He knew we were stale—and they've been state champions two years. They'd have murdered us, the way we were going.

The first thing I did was telephone Helen. Because that meant that there were a couple of extra afternoons we could have, if she could get rid of her music lessons some way. Well, she said, wasn't it wonderful, her music teacher had a cold? And that seemed just like Fate.

Well, that was a great week and we were so happy. We went to the movies five times, and once Mrs. Sharon let us take her car. She knew I didn't have a driver's license, but, of course, I've driven ever since I was thirteen and she said it was all right. She was funny—sometimes she'd be awfully kind and friendly to you and sometimes she'd be like a piece of dry ice. She was that way with Mr. Sharon too. But it was a wonderful ride. We got stuff out of the kitchen— the cook's awfully sold on Helen—and drove way out in the country. And we found an old house, with the windows gone, on top of a hill, and parked the car and took the stuff up to the house and ate it there. There weren't any chairs or tables but we pretended there were.

We pretended it was our house, after we were married. I'll never forget that. She'd even brought paper napkins and paper plates and she set two places on the floor.

"Well, Charles," she said, sitting opposite me, with her feet tucked under, "I don't suppose you remember the days we were both in school."

"Sure," I said—she was always much quicker pretending things than I was—"I remember all right. That was before Tot Pickens got to be President." And we both laughed.

"It seems very distant in the past to me—we've been married so long," she said, as if she really believed it. She looked at me.

"Would you mind turning off the radio, dear?" she said. "This modern music always gets on my nerves."

"Have we got a radio?" I said.

"Of course, Chuck."

"Gee, I'm glad," I said. I went and turned it off.

"Of course, if you want to listen to the late market reports—" she said just like Mrs. Sharon.

"Nope," I said. "The market—uh—closed firm today. Up twenty-six points."

"That's quite a long way up, isn't it?"

"Well the country's perfectly sound at heart, in spite of this damfool Congress," I said, like Father.

She lowered her eyes a minute, just like her mother, and pushed her plate away.

"I'm not very hungry tonight," she said. "You won't mind if I go upstairs?"

"Aw, don't be like that," I said. It was too much like her mother.

"I was just seeing if I could," she said. "But I never will, Chuck."

"I'll never tell you you're nervous, either," I said, "I—oh, gosh!"

She grinned and it was all right. "Mr. Ashland and I have never had a serious dispute in our wedded lives," she said—and everybody knows who runs that family. "We just talk things over calmly and reach a satisfactory conclusion, usually mine."

"Say, what kind of house have we got?"

"It's a lovely house," she said. "We've got radios in every room and lots of servants. We've got a regular movie projector and a library full of good classics and there's always something in the icebox. I've got a shoe closet."

"A what?"

"A shoe closet. All my shoes are on tipped shelves, like Mother's. And all my dresses are on those padded hangers. And I say to the maid, 'Elise, Madam will wear the new French model today.'"

"What are my clothes on?" I said. "Christmas trees?"

"Well," she said. "You've got lots of clothes and dogs. You smell of pipes and the open and something called Harrisburg tweed."

"I do not," I said. "I wish I had a dog. It's a long time since Jack."

"Oh, Chuck, I'm sorry," she said.

"Oh, that's all right," I said. "He was getting old and his ear was always bothering him. But he was a good pooch. Go ahead."

"Well," she said, "of course we give parties—"

"Cut the parties," I said.

"Chuck! They're grand ones!"

"I'm a homebody," I said. "Give me—er—my

wife and my little family and say, how many kids have we got anyway?"

She counted on her fingers. "Seven."

"Good Lord," I said.

"Well, I always wanted seven. You can make it three, if you like."

"Oh, seven's all right, I suppose," I said. "But don't they get awfully in the way?"

"No," she said. "We have governesses and tutors and send them to boarding school."

"O.K.," I said. "But it's a strain on the old man's pocketbook, just the same."

"Chuck, will you ever talk like that? Chuck, this is when we're rich." Then suddenly, she looked sad. "Oh, Chuck, do you suppose we ever will?" she said.

"Why, sure," I said.

"I wouldn't mind if it were only a dump," she said. "I could cook for you. I keep asking Hilda how she makes things."

I felt awfully funny. I felt as if I were going to cry.

"We'll do it," I said. "Don't you worry."

"Oh, Chuck, you're a comfort," she said.

I held her for a while. It was like holding something awfully precious. It wasn't mush or that way. I know what that's like too.

"It takes so long to get old," she said. "I wish I could grow up tomorrow. I wish we both could."

"Don't you worry," I said. "It's going to be all right."

We didn't say much, going back in the car,

but we were happy enough. I thought we passed Miss Eagles at the turn. That worried me a little because of the driver's license. But, after all, Mrs. Sharon had said we could take the car.

We wanted to go back again, after that, but it was too far to walk and that was the only time we had the car. Mrs. Sharon was awfully nice about it, but she said, thinking it over, maybe we'd better wait till I got a license. Well, Father didn't want me to get one till I was seventeen, but I thought he might come around. I didn't want to do anything that would get Helen in a jam with her family. That shows how careful I was of her. Or thought I was.

All the same, we decided we'd do something to celebrate if we won the St. Matthew's game. We thought it would be fun if we could get a steak and cook supper out somewhere—something like that. Of course we could have done it easily enough with a gang, but we didn't want a gang. We wanted to be alone together, the way we'd been at the house. That was all we wanted. I don't see what's wrong about that. We even took home the paper plates, so as not to litter things up.

Boy, that was a game! We beat them 58-54 and it took an extra period and I thought it would never end. That five-point lead they had looked as big as the Rocky Mountains all the first half. And they gave me the full cheer with nine Peterses when we tied them up. You don't forget things like that.

Afterwards, Mr. Grant had a kind of spread for

the team at his house and a lot of people came in. Kerry had driven down from State to see the game and that made me feel pretty swell. And what made me feel better yet was his taking me aside and saying, "Listen, kid, I don't want you to get a swelled head, but you did a good job. And, just remember this. Don't let anybody talk you out of going to State. You'll like it up there." And Mr. Grant heard him and laughed and said, "Well, Peters, I'm not recruiting. But your brother might think about some of the Eastern colleges." It was all like the kind of dream you have when you can do anything. It was wonderful.

Only Helen wasn't there because the only girls were older girls. I'd seen her for a minute, right after the game, and she was fine, but it was only a minute. I wanted to tell her about that big St. Matthews forward and—oh everything. Well, you like to talk things over with your girl.

Father and Mother were swell but they had to go on to some big wingding at the country club. And Kerry was going there with Sheila Coe. But Mr. Grant said he'd run me back to the house in his car and he did. He's a great guy. He made jokes about my being the infant phenomenon of basketball, and they were good jokes too. I didn't mind them. But, all the same, when I'd said good night to him and gone into the house, I felt sort of let down.

I knew I'd be tired the next day, but I didn't feel sleepy yet. I was too excited. I wanted to talk to somebody. I wandered around downstairs and wondered if Ida were still up. Well, she wasn't, but she'd left half a chocolate cake, covered over, on the kitchen table, and a note on top of it, "Congratulations to Mister Charles Peters." Well that was awfully nice of her and I ate some. Then I turned the radio on and got the time signal—eleven—and some music. But still I didn't feel like hitting the hay.

So I thought I'd call up Helen and then I thought—probably she's asleep and Hilda or Mrs. Sharon will answer the phone and be sore. And then I thought—well, anyhow, I could go over and walk around the block and look at her house. I'd get some fresh air out of it, anyway, and it would be a little like seeing her.

So I did—and it was a swell night—cool and a lot of stars—and I felt like a king, walking over. All the lower part of the Sharon house was dark, but a window upstairs was lit. I knew it was her window. I went around back of the driveway and whistled once—the whistle we made up. I never expected her to hear.

But she did, and there she was at the window smiling. She made motions that she'd come down to the side door.

Honestly, it took my breath away when I saw her. She had on a kind of yellow thing over her night clothes and she looked so pretty. Her feet were so pretty in those slippers. You almost expected her to be carrying one of those animals kids like—she looked young enough. I know I oughtn't to have gone into the house. But we didn't think anything about it—we were just glad to see each other. We hadn't had any sort of chance to talk over the game.

We sat in front of the fire in the living room and she went out to the kitchen and got us cookies and milk. I wasn't really hungry, but it was like that time at the house eating with her. Mr. and Mrs. Sharon were at the country club, too, so we weren't disturbing them or anything. We turned off the lights because there was plenty of light from the fire and Mr. Sharon's one person who can't stand having extra lights burning. Dad's that way about saving string.

It was quiet and lovely and the firelight made shadows on the ceiling. We talked a lot and then we just sat, each of us knowing the other was there. And the room got quieter and quieter and I'd told her about the game and I didn't feel excited or jumpy any more—just rested and happy. And then I knew by her breathing that she was asleep and I put my arm around her for just a minute, because it was wonderful to hear that quiet breathing and know it was hers. I was going to wake her in a minute. I didn't realize how tired I was myself.

And then we were back in that house in the country and it was our home and we ought to have been happy. But something was wrong because there still wasn't any glass in the windows and a wind kept blowing through them and we tried to shut the doors but they wouldn't shut. It drove Helen distracted and we were both running through the house, trying to shut the doors, and we were cold and afraid. Then the sun rose outside the windows, burning and yellow and so big it covered the sky. And with the sun was a horrible, weeping voice.

It was Mrs. Sharon's, saying, "Oh, good Lord! Oh, no. I can't believe it!"

I didn't know what had happened for a minute when I woke. And then I did and it was awful. Mrs. Sharon was saying "Oh, Helen—I trusted you . . ." and looking as if she were going to faint. And Mr. Sharon looked at her for a minute and his face was horrible and he said, "Bred in the bone," and she looked as if he'd hit her. Then he said to Helen—

Well, now, I don't want to think of any of it any more. Everything is spoiled. Miss Eagles saw us going to that house in the country and she said horrible things. They made Helen sick and she hasn't been back at school. There isn't any way I can see her. And if I could, it would be spoiled. We'd be thinking about the things they said.

I don't know how many of the people know at school. But Tot Pickens passed me a note. And, that afternoon, I caught him behind his house. I'd have broken his nose if they hadn't pulled me off. I meant to. Mother cried when she heard about it and Dad took me into his room and talked to me. He said you can't lick the whole town. But I will lick anybody like Tot Pickens. Dad and Mother have been all right. But they say things about Helen and that's almost worse. They're for me because I'm their son. But they don't understand.

I thought I could talk to Kerry, but I can't.

He was nice, but he looked at me such a funny way. I don't know—sort of impressed. It wasn't the way I wanted him to look. But he's been decent. He comes down almost every weekend and we play catch in the yard.

You see, I just go to school and back now. They want me to go with the gang, the way I did, but I can't do that. Not after Tot. Of course my marks are a lot better because I've got more time to study now. But it's lucky I haven't got Miss Eagles, though Dad made her apologize. I couldn't recite to her.

I think Mr. Grant knows because he asked me to his house once and we had a conversation. Not about that, though I was terribly afraid he would. He showed me a lot of his old college things and the gold football he wears on his watch chain. He's got a lot of interesting things.

Then he got talking somehow, about history and things like that and how times had changed. Why, there were kings and queens who got married younger than Helen and me. Only now we lived longer and had a lot more to learn. So it couldn't happen now. "It's civilization," he said. "And all civilization's against nature. But I suppose we've got to have it. Only sometimes it isn't easy." Well somehow or other, that made me feel less lonely. Before that I'd been feeling I was the only person on earth who'd ever felt that way.

I'm going to Colorado, this summer, to a ranch, and next year, I'll go East to school. Mr. Grant says he thinks I can make the basketball team, if I work hard enough, though I don't think it's as big a game in the East as it is with us. Well, I'd like to show them something. It would be some satisfaction. He says not to be too fresh at first, but I won't be that.

It's a boys' school and there aren't even women teachers. And, maybe afterwards, I could be a professional basketball player or something, where you don't have to see women at all. Kerry says I'll get over that; but I won't. They all sound like Mrs. Sharon to me now when they laugh.

They're going to send Helen to a convent—I found out that. Maybe they'll let me see her before she goes: But, if we do, it will be all wrong and in front of people and everybody pretending. I sort of wish they won't—though I want to, terribly. When her mother took her upstairs that night—she wasn't the same Helen. She looked at me as if she were afraid of me. And no matter what they do for us now, they can't fix that.